THE AURIGA PROJECT

THE AURIGA PROJECT

TRANSLOCATOR TRILOGY BOOK ONE

M.G. HERRON

MG Publishing LLC

Cover design: Beaulistic Book Services

Stock photo model: Claire Jones

ISBN-13: 978-1517039790
ISBN-10: 1517039797

First Edition: September 2015
Second Edition: July 2017

A GUIDE TO THE PRONUNCIATION OF NAMES

Though ample evidence suggests there existed a wide variety of languages and dialects among the ancient people of Central America, this author based the language of the *Kakuli* people on Yucatec Maya, the most commonly spoken—and well documented—Mayan language today.

Characters names were mostly invented. Specific words, when borrowed, were taken from modern Yucatec Maya dictionaries and archaeological texts. Where English transliterations varied, spelling was chosen for consistency and simplicity. The lovely sound of the Mayan language is poorly expressed with English letters, so a rough pronunciation guide follows.

NAMES

Citlali
[Kit-LA-li]

Dambu
[DAHM-boo]

Ixchel
[EESH-chel]

Kakul
[KA-cool]

Rakulo
[RAHK-oo-lo]

Tilak
[Tee-LAHK]

Uchben Na
[OOCH-ben Nah]

Xucha
[SHOO-cha]

TABLE OF CONTENTS

1
THE DEMONSTRATION

ELIANA TRIED HER best to look elegant in a black cocktail dress as she drifted across the lawn to greet arriving guests. When her cheeks ached from smiling, and the portion of the quad decorated for the demonstration began to fill up, she adjusted centerpieces and worried the back of one hand with the thumb of the other. Everything had been cross-checked and triple-confirmed: the catering, the press arrangements, the invite-only guest list. Eliana didn't mind the intensive planning required for a big event like this. Organizing and fitting came fairly naturally to a trained archaeologist—she could make sense of that kind of chaos, the kind you could cut and move and change and see.

But all that work was done now. And despite hiring the most capable event planner she could find in Austin, Texas—who at this very moment directed her staff through a wireless microphone like a conductor commanding an orchestra—Eliana fidgeted nervously. How her hands could remain so steady holding ancient fossils yet shake in the presence of her husband's colleagues, she would never understand.

A few pointedly underdressed venture capitalists, several politicians with plastic smiles, and a group of Fisk Industries' brightest minds lounged against the open bar. Above them, a wide screen played clips of rocket launches from the Lunar Terraform Alliance's early missions, the ones that had established the Lunar Station and begun construction of the first biodome. Amon had chosen the launch clips as an homage to the halcyon early days of the international organization, when everything was possible and physical limitations were taken as challenges to be bested—the days before the energy crisis, before the failed resupply missions, before the primary biodome ruptured in a series of violent explosions that set the terraform initiative back years and cost dozens of lives.

The Auriga Project was a rallying cry for a return to those early days, her husband, Amon, had explained. His radical invention was a way back for the organization, a renewed hope representing a brighter future.

"*Hallo,*" a portly gentleman said. The heavily accented greeting pulled Eliana back to the present. She smiled as she recognized him from the guest list she had memorized. He was the president of Hermann Buch, GmbH, a major stakeholder in Amon's project.

"*Guten Abend, Herr Buch,*" Eliana said.

"Ah!" he replied, his bristle brush mustache wiggling with excitement. "*Sprechst du Deutsch?*"

"*Viel bisschen,*" Eliana said. She struggled through rusty German phrases she hadn't practiced since the year she'd spent abroad in Europe during her undergraduate studies. She'd had reason to use other languages in her travels since, but German wasn't one of them. Meanwhile, Diane, the event planner, weaved toward her through the crowd.

She mouthed "five minutes" to Eliana over the old German's shoulder. When the director of the Lunar Terraform Alliance, Dr. Enzo Badeux, approached them, Herr Buch switched to English, the common language between them. Eliana excused herself a moment later and walked across the quad toward the engineering building where Amon was getting ready.

The Fisk Industries campus consisted of half a dozen buildings of vastly different architectural styles, arranged in a semicircle around a central lawn. In a former life, a small private university had called the campus home, and the lawn was known as a quad. When the university filed for bankruptcy, Amon purchased the land and decided to keep the old Gothic Revival-era buildings. They were made of gray stone with vaulted doorways, carved balustrades, and faux ramparts. Green vines crawled up them, carefully maintained so as not to cause structural damage to the aging stone. Belying their outward appearances, the buildings' innards had been modernized and ran on completely renewable energy—mostly solar, fitting for the largest researcher and manufacturer of consumer-friendly solar generation technology in the United States.

In stark contrast to the Gothic style, the headquarters building stood at the north end of the quad, imposing and modern. Two sheer glass walls swept inward and met at steel-framed double doors. Bold silver letters atop the entryway spelled out the company name, *Fisk Industries*.

Eliana was within sight of the lobby entrance when Senator Caldwell parted ways with a straight-mouthed, short-haired woman to intercept her.

"Mrs. Fisk," the senator said, pocketing the woman's business card. Eliana caught a glimpse of the name on the front of the card as it disappeared into his pocket. It read, *HAWKWOOD*. "Quite the event! You look splendid, by the way."

She thought she looked nice as well, but she recognized his compliment as a strategic opening.

"Thank you," she said.

"Wes McManis tells me you're an accomplished archeologist."

She tried to keep her face neutral. *And how much I'd rather be on the coast of Turkey dusting off the ruins of Ephesus than talking to you! No*, she reprimanded herself. She had chosen to leave that life behind. She had volunteered for this job. She forced a smile. "That's correct."

"I'd love to tell you about our efforts to raise money for the Young Scholars Association, if you're interested. It would be great to have someone like you involved."

She barely repressed a sigh. Wes McManis had a big mouth. One of these days, someone would want her for her own work, and not for her husband's money. It seemed that day was not today.

"I'd love to hear more," she said. "But I really must be going. The demonstration is about to begin."

"No worries! No trouble at all. Don't let me hold you up," the senator said with a smile.

She'd be fooling herself to think that would discourage him from trying again later.

Several more people took the opportunity to intercept Eliana, fishing for hints of the demonstration to come. She carefully parried their questions. The only facts Fisk Industries had confirmed in the press releases leading up to the event were that Amon's invention was the result of ten years of work, and that it would "change the face of space travel forever." The PR agency's words, not hers. She would have been more subtle.

Finally, she strode past the portable stage and crossed to the glass-fronted face of the headquarters building. As her quick steps rang on the tile floors, she checked the clock on the lobby wall.

Crap, she thought. *Late already.*

She rotated her wedding band on her finger. Normally, she wore her diamond engagement ring to a big event like this—Amon's mother's ring, a family heirloom. But she'd lost that classic gem in Cairo last year along with the tattered shreds of her once-promising career.

She didn't realize the ring was missing until the plane lifted from the runway in Cairo.

She begged the flight attendants to halt the plane. They seemed to be sympathetic to her situation and relayed the message to the cockpit, but the pilot refused to turn around.

When she got home, Eliana dropped her bags in her room and collapsed onto the bed. She pulled the blanket over her head to close out the world.

By the time Amon returned from his business trip to New York, Eliana was a complete wreck. Rock 'n' roll blared from the house-wide speaker system. Her suitcase and purse seemed to have exploded in their bedroom, and the trail of debris led him to the master bath.

Amon turned down the music as he entered. He sat on the edge of the tub. "Sweetheart, the water is freezing."

She tipped a wine bottle to her mouth and took a swig without lifting her head from the edge of the porcelain tub. "Still feels pretty nice to me," she slurred.

"How long have you been in here?"

"An hour or six, who cares?"

The tears she'd managed to fend off with the wine and rock 'n' roll came rushing back. Amon's face went all blurry. His warm, rough hands caressed her damp cheeks. She lifted her free hand from the tub and clutched his fingers.

"I lost your mother's ring," she sobbed against his chest. "I called the hotel a million times, but they can't find it."

"It's just a ring," he said, his voice thick. "I'll buy you a new one. Tell me what happened in Cairo."

She took a big, shaking breath. "All the supposed cultural heritage organizations in the Middle East care about are their tourist traps. Whatever. I'm tired of the desert anyways."

"What about your connections in Belize? Have you reached out to any of your old professors? I'm sure something will come up if you keep looking."

She sniffed. "I'm not sure I want to."

"Come on," he said, lifting her by the elbow. "Let's get you into something warm." He helped her out of the tub, across the cold bathroom floor, and into bed.

The next morning, Amon insisted on going out for brunch. His cell phone rang in the car on the way to the restaurant.

"Hello?"

"Hey," Lucas said. His voice came through the phone, tinny and small but discernible. "How'd your meeting with the LTA go?"

"Yeah, it went great. Thanks for checking in."

"Good to hear. Negotiations are progressing quickly on my end as well. This week, I spoke to Audi, GE, Hawkwood, and Facebook about the design for the new industrial solar cells. They all seem very interested in what we're developing."

"Excellent. I knew you were the right man to put in charge."

"Thanks," Lucas said.

"Listen, I'm on my way out to eat with Eliana. Can we catch up later?"

"You bet," Lucas said. "Bye for now."

At brunch, Eliana drank black coffee and nibbled at a bagel while Amon gestured excitedly across the table. "The LTA fast-tracked the real-world trials," he said. "We have a timeline now. If everything goes smoothly, we'll be able to announce the program in six months. A year, tops."

"Wow," she said. "That's great news."

Amon leaned in. "And then they want to do a public demonstration, to rekindle positive interest in the organization. After waiting so long, I can't say I'm not relieved. Though it's surreal. I've been working on it for so long that I forget the rest of the world doesn't even know it exists. You and I do, but they don't. There's probably going to be some pushback from the media, at least initially."

"I bet," she said.

"We need a code name for the announcement—something that captures the imagination and gets people talking about it without revealing what it is. I want it to sound heroic."

"Hmm. How about the Auriga Project?"

"What's that mean?"

"It means charioteer in Latin. In Greek mythology, it's named after the ruler of ancient Athens, King Erichthonius, a famous charioteer. Also, the Chinese incorporated the stars of Auriga into several constellations, among them the celestial emperor's chariots."

"That's perfect," Amon said. He hesitated for a moment then whispered, "The idea of all the media attention makes me nervous."

"I think you can handle it."

He paused. A smirk spread across his face.

"I know that look," she said. "What?"

"I want you to be a part of it."

"Of course I'll be there."

"Not simply be there," he said. "Be *involved*. I've been thinking, how would you like to help me plan the event? God knows we could use you right now. The company is growing faster than ever. Hey, maybe it would even help get your mind off other things?"

Where Latin words came easy, this suggestion sank slowly into Eliana's hung-over brain. When it did, a smothering foam of disappointment pressed against her diaphragm. She was momentarily thankful she didn't have much of an appetite this morning.

I'm well into my thirties, she mused bitterly, *and I've failed to make any important discoveries in my field. No hominid remains for me, no discoveries that change the way the scientific community interprets our ancient past. My legacy consists of many long, hot dig trips and one struggling field research organization that can't get funded.*

People no longer seemed to care about historical monuments or ancient artifacts like they used to. The sense that there was nothing left to discover permeated the field of archaeology. She and her colleagues all knew there was more money in tearing down ancient buildings than preserving or studying them. Each year, a few more said goodbye.

Amon knew better than to offer her money. He'd done so before, several times—she always turned him down. He proved himself once again to be too clever for his own good by offering her a job instead. She saw the warmth in his eyes. He really meant it. So she didn't give him a straight answer.

"I'll consider it," she said, knowing that it would mean taking a sabbatical of sorts, a leave of absence, if not giving up on her fund-raising efforts altogether. She knew from watching her colleagues' lives diverge how easily that could turn into giving up on the field entirely.

"You plan amazing parties."

"I wouldn't call getting your Stanford buddies drunk on the weekends 'amazing,' but I'll take the compliment."

They laughed. He took her hand and stroked the tan line on her finger where her wedding ring used to be.

After giving herself a few more days of moping around, she walked into Amon's office at Fisk Industries and announced that she'd be taking the job. "Part time," she insisted. "To see if Fisk Industries is a good fit for me."

But Eliana could never do anything by halves. She immersed herself in VIP guest lists, interviews with event planning companies, and press releases—giving herself over to the new role completely.

She found Amon, Lucas, and Reuben talking business in the middle of the marble-floored lobby.

"Ah, here she is," said Lucas Lamotte, chief financial officer of Fisk Industries. His immaculate three-piece charcoal suit was as finely tailored as his beard, sharp-edged against his smooth skin. "We were keeping your husband company until you arrived."

"Lucas," Eliana said, inclining her head in greeting. His hair was a shade darker than the last time she saw him. He must have dyed it fresh for the cameras, a habit he'd recently acquired to hide the salt and pepper that had begun to creep in.

Gray had begun to fleck her husband's hair as well. The last two years had been hard on them both.

"Hullo, Mrs. Fisk," Reuben rumbled from her right. Smile lines creased the old engineer's face, radiating out from his mouth and the corners of his warm, green eyes. She enjoyed Reuben's company, and reminded herself once again to come up with an excuse to spend time with him outside of work-related functions.

"Reuben, you look handsome," she said.

"Thank you, dear," he said, running his fingers through his hair. His normally wild and unkempt gray-blond strands were slicked back for the occasion.

"We'll leave you to it then," said Lucas, clapping his hands together.

Reuben nodded to the couple and followed Lucas out, but at his own pace.

"It's time," Eliana said once she was alone with her husband.

"Thank God," said Amon. "I can't wait to get this over with. I sweated through my tuxedo ages ago."

"Don't worry, you look great." Eliana took a blue handkerchief from Amon's breast pocket and dabbed at his neck.

Amon wore a tuxedo they had purchased especially for tonight. It was the only tux he had ever owned. Like Reuben, Amon was a man of science, and formal dress remained firmly outside of his comfort zone. Eliana loved how he looked in the fitted attire, bow tie and all.

"Do you want to go over the stage directions one more time?" she asked.

"I have something for you."

"What? *Now*?" Eliana said, distracted from her original intention.

"We've waited years for this, what's another five minutes?" He withdrew something from his coat pocket—a velvet box that fit in the palm of his hand.

Eliana took it with shaking hands and eased open the lid. She gasped. "Amon... my God, it's beautiful."

Amon carefully lifted a silver ring with a large diamond, black as night, from the velvet cushion. He slipped it onto her finger.

She tilted her hand this way and that. It fit perfectly. The smoky translucence of the stone gave it a deceptive depth—she gazed into it and saw tiny stars, microscopic galaxies, swimming in its core.

"It looks just like your mother's ring, except for the gemstone... how did you find a diamond this color?"

Amon's mouth turned up at one corner. "I saw how upset you were after you lost the ring in Cairo, so I had it remade from old photographs of my parents. Except for the carbonado—that's what the black diamond's called. It was harvested from a meteorite."

"It's incredible," she said. "Thank you."

Amon gathered her into his arms. "It's I who should be thanking you. For being here with me tonight, and for working so hard to put this whole thing together. It means so much to me."

"Please. I had help! Diane is a miracle worker, I'm telling you." Her heart warmed at his praise. And yet, deep down, she did not register contentment. Putting together the party did not give her the satisfaction she had expected, merely relief that it would soon be over. She missed the rich history of archaeology work, the possibility of joy that lay dormant in even the most tedious excavation.

"You're being modest, as usual," Amon said. "Without you, none of this would have been possible." He gestured not merely to the party outside, but to the lobby, the building, the campus and everything it represented.

Eliana smiled and took a deep breath. A curious thing had happened while she adjusted to working as a Fisk Industries employee. For one, she was glad to be able to spend more time with Amon after being on the road so often. Her travels and his work schedule had been erratic before.

More importantly, their careers had never crossed paths until now. Working with him every day introduced a new aspect to a ten-year-old marriage that had grown, if not stale, then perhaps complacent. She supposed both of them were at fault to a certain extent.

She forgot all that when she saw how Amon's employees smiled when he walked into a room, how his team of engineers looked up to him, and how the new hires, specially the interns, spoke together in hushed whispers after a chance meeting with "Amonfisk," and how they always called him "Amonfisk"—one word—like he was a rock star.

Their adoration for him had ignited a spark of passion in her heart again, something she hadn't felt in recent years of their marriage.

And yet some part of her knew she would never be content if her life revolved around planning events—even important ones like this. It wasn't enough to make her truly happy.

"I love you, Amon," Eliana said. "And I'm so proud of what you've accomplished."

"But?"

"But I miss my job. It's been so great getting to spend time together for a change, but I'm not ready to give up on it yet."

"I would never ask you to."

"You mean that?"

"Of course. I'll fire you right now, put you on a plane to Greece...or Turkey! I'll buy a pyramid and ship it home brick by brick if that's what you want, darling."

Eliana laughed. In that moment, she fell in love with him all over again. "I know you would."

She stepped back out of his embrace and rotated the new ring on her finger, thoughtful this time instead of anxious. She imagined how, once the media got over the initial shock of Amon's announcement, their lives might once again return to normal. Eliana would step down from her role as professional wife and resume her hunt for grant money to build a new organization. Though her life had taken a yearlong detour, she felt a passion for dig trips and old ruins and unanswered questions about ancient cultures resurfacing. She was excited and scared and in love, and it made her feel alive.

"Well," she said when she remembered to breathe. "Are you ready?"

"No way," Amon said. "Once I get out there, I'll be fine. It's this next part I hate." He tugged at his damp collar with one finger.

"I know," she said as she took his hand.

2
THE AURIGA PROJECT

A HUNDRED BURSTS OF light blinded Amon as he stepped through the doors. Photographers crowded around them, pushing cameras into their personal space. He tensed at each flash, involuntarily gripping Eliana's hand tighter. She kept moving. By focusing on putting one foot in front of the other, he did, too.

Eventually, they ascended a set of metal stairs, which were then removed to clear the area for the demonstration. The swarm of photographers regrouped behind the rope delimiting the media area at the foot of the stage.

Onstage, with the cameras at a reasonable distance, Amon took a deep breath. He patted Eliana's hand and left her next to Reuben, who stood clapping with Lucas, Wes McManis, Herr Buch, Dr. Badeux, and a few other LTA representatives who had flown in from Europe, Asia, and Africa. As Amon approached the microphone, they took their seats.

The audience followed suit, and the applause tapered off. Amon continued to sweat beneath the glare of overhead lights, but there was nothing to be done about it now. He glanced over the crowd as he made his way to the microphone. He had decided against a podium, so as not to obstruct anyone's view. Even so, with the quad full of people, for a moment he felt uncomfortably exposed.

Taking another deep breath, he fought down his anxiety. Dusk faded slowly into night as several hundred pairs of eyes looked expectantly toward him. He waited until the murmuring died down to a whisper. Then he waited a moment longer. So much effort had led to this moment that he felt it deserved to be savored. He stood up a little straighter.

When the audience began to fidget, Amon cleared his throat and spoke into the silence. "Ten years ago, Fisk Industries began work on a transportation project with the Lunar Terraform Alliance. It's been a long and difficult journey. There have been setbacks; there have been failures. Some people out there—some of you here tonight—told me that I was wasting my time. That we were throwing money away trying to accomplish the impossible.

"I thought so myself, at first. But after working closely with the scientists at the LTA, after getting to know the astronauts and engineers that brave death on a daily basis to build and maintain the Lunar Station's three biodomes, I came around to a new way of thinking."

Even as he spoke, a low rumble caused the entire quad to vibrate. Without turning to look, Amon knew that a semi-circle of sod behind the stage had telescoped open, and a two-hundred-foot-tall, arch-shaped array of silicone and metal nodes had climbed skyward behind him.

"Fortunately," he went on, his voice barely carrying over the audience who murmured in surprise, "the advances we've made in particle physics over the past several decades have given us new knowledge, and we've applied it to solve an old problem. As they say, we stand on the shoulders of giants."

The base of the arch rose until it was level with Amon's feet, seamlessly extending the stage. Centered beneath the arch, a sphere of concentric blue-green alloy rings encircled a slightly raised platform. The sphere of rings was twenty-five feet in diameter and held in place with magnets so they could spin freely. Rotating slightly, the rings came to rest so that a space tall enough for an SUV to drive through conveniently opened onto the ramp leading up to the platform in the sphere.

The choreography was timed perfectly. Amon likened the visual effect of the entire contrivance to a piece of modern art—sparse and powerful, delicate and surreal. With the glass-walled flagship building of Fisk Industries visible through its empty spaces, it filled one with a great hope...and a great sense of skepticism. To most, space travel meant a rocket or a plane, a flying machine with wings and thrusters. But this?

Amon took the microphone from its stand. As he crossed the stage, he reached out and let his fingers skim the cool alloy rings whose contours he knew so well. He moved past the sphere and stopped in front of an arrangement of displays: two floor-mounted holographic projectors, and a wide glass touch screen. The other screens arranged around the quad, the ones that had been showing his favorite rocket launch clips, faded to black and were replaced with a video feed of the pockmarked lunar surface and a concave reflection of a biodome in the background.

Amon traced the multiple redundant power cables below the stage in his mind. They were hardwired, connecting the entire apparatus to the lab below ground, and from there to the particle accelerator that powered the Hopper. The official name was the Translocator, but in the years before it had an official title, he and Reuben had begun referring to it as the Hopper—and that's how he still thought of it.

As they had rehearsed, Reuben rose from his seat next to Eliana and joined Amon at the console. He powered up the holo displays with a sharp upward motion of both arms. The holos kicked on, illuminating a model of the arch in miniature, and controls like the cockpit of a fighter jet arrayed themselves in the air.

Amon continued his speech, moving back to the center of the stage. "The biggest obstacle faced by the team of scientists and engineers at the Lunar Station has always been to establish a reliable supply chain. They've experienced no end of problems in their effort to get the supplies they need, when they need them. As a result, many lives have been lost—to equipment failures, to accidents, to materials and tools forced to perform past their intended lifecycles of use. Furthermore, the energy crisis on Earth has made an impact on all our lives, not least our ability to continue spending billions building and launching inefficient rockets. As a result, the Lunar Station's original plans have been pushed back decades from their original projections."

Reuben made a few gestures, and the particle accelerator came to life beneath them. As energy flowed into the stabilizing poles of the arch, a thin keening noise pierced the air like the sound of a camera flash charging, audible across the entire campus.

The audience tensed and shifted in their seats. They exchanged worried glances. Amon could understand their reaction. If he didn't know what to expect, that sound would have been…unsettling.

"The breakthrough in molecular reassembly made by Ortega's team at the European Space Agency opened our eyes to the possibilities. Building on their research, we have constructed a mechanism capable of translocating objects directly to the lunar surface."

Under the spotlights, Amon saw everyone in the crowd glance around uneasily. Molecular reassembly and translocation were touchy subjects. They were the reasons the LTA had insisted on keeping the Auriga Project under wraps until the process had been stabilized.

First discovered in a secret lab in Germany in the 1930s, Nazi fringe scientists pioneered the molecular reassembly process. Nearly a century later, when the experiment was finally declassified by the German parliament, it was reproduced on a small scale by Ortega's team at the ESA and in private labs around the world. The ESA upgraded its experiments to live subjects—lab mice—too quickly and were shut down shortly after animal rights activists learned that the subjects were being reassembled with missing limbs, with absent organs, or not at all.

The scientific community caught wind of it and hurriedly canned all the open projects. Major publications like *WIRED* and *Popular Science* and the academic community as a whole lambasted the ESA for green-lighting those projects, and deemed molecular reassembly to be "unsafe and irresponsible."

Since then, no one had attempted to recreate the process, let alone attempt it on such a large scale.

Until now.

Amon was well aware of the scientific trail of errors he proposed to inherit when the project began. His experiments were classified and funded by the LTA, so he had the buffer he needed to conduct them in secret. More to his advantage, an engineering problem could be solved without putting any lives at risk. No activists would be picketing his lab as long as he didn't test the process on living subjects. Instead, his team focused on transmitting homogenous uniform materials, and then upgraded to mixed nonorganics like glass and metal and plastic and clay. Eventually, they were able to translocate batteries and, finally, computer parts, flawlessly. They'd moved into organic trials shortly after that—plants and wood and dirt, then small creatures. Unlike Ortega's team, they never had any issues with lab mice. The activists could complain if they wanted, but now it was too late. They hadn't had any failed translocations in years.

"Ladies and gentlemen," Amon said, gesturing to the machine that towered over him, the fruit the past ten years of his life were about to bear, "I give you the Auriga Project, the future of space travel, the Translocator."

A halfhearted round of applause rose from the crowd. He had expected hesitation. They would have to see it to believe it.

"We've taken every precaution for the purposes of this demonstration," Amon went on. "When Ortega's team first pioneered the molecular reassembly process, it was far from safe. We know that, and have made significant advances. Now, a man can step through the Translocator and come out on the surface of the moon as easily as he can walk across the street. We've met with the approval of an LTA oversight committee, a board of top-notch scientists picked from all over the world—many of whom are here with us tonight. So we can all witness the demonstration, we'll be using a twelfth-generation rover named Carbon to help us out. He's waiting in the lab below. Reuben, would you bring him up here, please?"

Reuben's fingers twitched, and a series of glyphs lit the top of the screen, spelling out the parameters for the translocation. The great arch came to life. The keening noise amplified its pitch and intensity until it climbed above the audible range for the human ear and went silent. Blue-white sparks of energy flickered between nodes of the arch.

The sphere of concentric rings around the platform spun, collecting the energy from the outer arch and concentrating it inside the sphere. The sphere spun, blurred, and radiated a soft turquoise brightness.

Then the light was gone, the rings wound down, and a lunar rover appeared on the platform—its squat, wheeled form perfectly intact.

The crowd exploded with applause. Reuben inputted a few more commands on the console and the rover rolled to Amon's side.

Amon tried to hide his smile. This was a parlor trick compared to what was coming next. The appearance of the rover had been meant to warm up the crowd and dispel their initial doubt. Carbon had merely been transported from the lab a few floors below ground. The surface of the moon, however, was hundreds of thousands of miles from Earth, and moving at an incredible velocity.

"Tonight, Carbon will be making the journey to the lunar surface. He's made this journey many times in our years of testing, but tonight is the first time he will do so in public. A team is waiting for him in the research biodome of the Lunar Station."

Reuben motioned, and a new set of parameters appeared. Amon waited for him to nod then said, "My wife, Eliana, will help me christen this maiden voyage. Sweetheart, if you'll do me the honor?" He held out his hand.

Eliana walked across the stage and took Amon's hand.

"Traditionally, you'd break a champagne bottle across the hull," Amon said to the audience. "But I don't know if that's recommended when we're working with electronics." When Eliana laughed, the crowd laughed along with her.

Amon and Eliana met Reuben at the control unit. As rehearsed, Eliana stood between her husband and Reuben in front of the screen.

Reuben keyed in a few commands, and a series of calculations scrolled up. Amon double checked Reuben's work as he did it, verifying energy levels coming in from the particle accelerator and calculating the moon's position, rotation, and velocity in real time. They didn't have to speak. Amon knew everything was going according to plan on Reuben's end by his grunts of approval.

When they were ready, Reuben verified radio communication with the lunar team then cleared the display and brought up a green *Initiate* button. The button was strictly for show and big enough for the cameras to make out.

Reuben nudged the button's digital image across the display so it was in front of Eliana. She reached out her left hand—her new ring glittered. When her fingers came into contact with the screen, she pulled her hand back sharply, as if she had been zapped by an electric shock. She rubbed her fingers and frowned.

"Are you okay?" Amon whispered into her ear, careful to hold the microphone away from his mouth.

"I'm fine," she said, quick to put a smile back on her face for the cameras. She moved a few steps from the display—not part of the stage directions they had rehearsed, but Amon was too distracted by what happened next to give it much thought.

The machine screamed as it came to life. The keening noise didn't go sub audible, but escalated into a banshee's screech. Electricity popped loudly across the arch, and great tree-like shapes of blue-white lightning shot into the air in every direction.

"Reuben, what's happening?" Amon shouted, turning back to the display. A graph that measured the energy output from the particle accelerator careened into the danger zone. Reuben gestured wildly, trying to regain control of the apparatus, but the holo controls were no longer responding to his increasingly frantic motions.

"It's unresponsive. Initiate emergency shutdown!"

Amon dropped the mic with a clunk that was swallowed in the chaos. He leaped over to the display, yanked out a tactile keyboard from the base of the screen, and began rapidly typing in override commands designed to short-circuit the translocation.

It didn't respond to those either.

"Cut the power!" Amon yelled. Reuben was already tearing at the floorboards to reach the power cables beneath them. Electricity saturated the air, causing Reuben's hair to stand on end and wave wildly.

Reuben held up the control unit's plug. Amon glanced up and saw the display was dead. The arch continued to thrum with energy.

"Shit!" Amon said, already knowing it was too late. The redundant power cables connecting the arch and the translocation platform to the particle accelerator meant that they would have to cut all the power cables to shut it down. And there wasn't enough time for that.

"Eliana!" Amon yelled, twisting frantically as he searched for her. The light radiating from the sphere of rings this time was blinding, a bright-white sun that outshone the spotlights fixed on the stage.

He shielded his eyes with one hand and squinted into the light. The chairs where Lucas and Wes had been seated were empty—they must have retreated from the stage when the Hopper malfunctioned. Did they take Eliana with them?

But then he spotted her, silhouetted against the great ball of light that emanated from the sphere.

He sprinted toward her only to stumble into something hard that tripped him and sent him sprawling to the deck. He felt the bar of the microphone stand beneath him as he pushed himself back up.

He juked around Carbon, the lunar rover. She was ten feet from him now. Eliana stretched her arm toward the sphere of light, reaching. She gasped, her mouth widening, as the expanding radiance engulfed her wrist.

Five feet away. He lifted his knees, pumped his arms, reached out to grab her. The light swallowed her elbow, her shoulder, half her body. A terrible dread lined Amon's stomach with steel wool.

Two feet. He jumped, reaching out. Instead of coming into contact with Eliana, he felt the light as a physical resistance pushing back at him like a viscous liquid.

The feeling of resistance retreated suddenly. He slammed into the unforgiving hardness of alloy rings, knocking the breath from his lungs.

Eliana. He gasped and writhed on the ground, shocked from the impact. *Where did she go?* Gritting his teeth against the pain, he pushed himself to his feet.

Red spots crowded his vision. When they cleared, he saw that the stage was illuminated by only the spotlights now, and bulbs flashed from the media pit. The horrible screeching noise had ceased, but shouts from the audience filled his hearing. He stood on the translocation platform inside the alloy rings.

Alone.

3
TWO MOONS AND A PURPLE SKY

ONE MINUTE, A thousand tiny blades lacerated Eliana's skin, like her body was being ripped to shreds. The next, she sat up on a hot beach and spat out sand.

The heavy, humid air intensified her sudden nausea. She tried to ignore it while she took in her surroundings.

The beach was too clean for the Gulf Coast, that was for sure. The humidity, too, seemed uncharacteristic for Texas, even on a sweltering summer evening. It reminded her of the time she and Amon had made the mistake of traveling to Cancún in the middle of July.

But it wasn't evening anymore. A blazing yellow sun high overhead beat her down with an oppressive heat.

Eliana shivered in cold sweats as her body adjusted to the rapid change in temperature.

"What the hell?" she said aloud. Hearing her own voice disperse in the thick air made her acutely aware of her isolation.

She slipped off her heels and tried to stand, biting back the flutter of panic that threatened to overtake her. Her legs wobbled, black spots crowded her vision, and she fell down with a groan.

As she lay there, fighting to remain conscious, it occurred to her that the fitted black dress and low strappy heels she had chosen for the demonstration were totally inappropriate for the beach. Even olive skin like hers would burn in a matter of minutes exposed to the fiery sun.

She laughed in spite of herself. She thought, *Do I not have more pressing concerns?*

"Where am I?" she said to no one.

She closed her eyes and forced herself to think rationally through what she had just experienced. One minute, she had been posing during the demonstration, with Amon by her side, trying to make sure the camera had a good angle on her hand—with her lovely new ring—while she pressed the *Initiate* button on the display. The next, something had tugged her toward the expanding sphere of light, her hand reaching out as if it had a will of its own.

The shock she'd taken from the display screen had numbed her hand completely when it zapped her. She cracked one eye and held her hand up to the light. It felt fine. Could the ring possibly have caused whatever went wrong? Looking at it now, it seemed not much different from any other diamond, except for the gem's unusual smoky depth.

When it had pulled her toward the brilliant sphere of light expanding from the translocation platform—and thinking about it, she became certain that some force had leashed her hand and drawn her to it—she remembered the diamond glowing with the same every-color radiance as the sphere. Was she imagining it, or had the gemstone somehow channeled the electricity that crackled through the air?

The instant of primal terror Eliana felt as the light washed over her was nothing compared to the binding knot of dread that found a seat in her gut now.

Refusing to let the fear take over, Eliana struggled to her feet once more, willing her knees to be steady, and surveyed her position.

She stood on a long stretch of beach that separated a dense green jungle on one side from a calm surf on the other. The ocean's flat expanse stretched all the way to the horizon, which, unless Eliana was mistaken, had a more pronounced curve than she was used to. Not ten yards from where she stood, purple waves washed onto the shore.

Eliana blinked and rubbed her oddly weary eyes. *Purple waves? Am I seeing things?*

She walked to the water's edge. It was beautifully translucent and—yes—a light purple in color. She turned her gaze to the cloudless sky. It was a similar shade of pale violet, reflecting the sea.

Or is it the other way around? Does the sea reflect the sky?

Gazing up, Eliana noticed two faint moons that hung in the cloudless firmament. One appeared to be significantly smaller than the other. A big bite had been taken out of the top right shoulder of the larger satellite. Both were roughly three-quarters full, but she had no way to tell if they were waxing or waning.

Her mind turned its gears again, coming to terms with the strangeness of her situation. Her nausea remained. She forced herself to be rational, thinking, *You're not in Kansas anymore, Dorothy*.

She also knew from her experience at dig sites that she needed two things to survive the heat: shade and water. Without them, she was a goner.

She dragged herself up the beach and sat in the sand dunes beneath two big floppy leaves at the edge of the jungle. Tiny insects swarmed around her sweaty neck and left red marks where they bit her. Since it was easily twenty degrees cooler in the shade, she determined not to let the bugs bother her while she allowed herself a moment to rest.

Though her situation was dire, Eliana felt a wave of sympathy for Amon. No doubt he was more panicked than she was about her disappearance. At least she knew she was alive. For all Amon knew, she had been vaporized, her molecules scattered to the winds. It seemed like nothing more than blind luck that she had landed on solid ground, somewhere with *water*—even purple water—instead of being teleported to cold, empty space. What little she understood of Amon's work made it abundantly clear which was the more likely scenario.

Amon would not approve of her sitting here, wallowing in self-pity and thinking about him. He would be out there running around, trying to find her, thinking up solutions to the problem instead of pouting. Reuben would be helping him. Lucas, too.

The media would be eating this up. She imagined the headline: "Famous Inventor's Wife Goes Missing in His Own Machine."

That wouldn't flummox him. He'd be searching for her. The least she could do was make sure she was alive when he got here.

With a new determination, Eliana slapped another bug on her neck. She glanced into the shadows in the jungle behind her. If she wasn't dressed for the beach, she certainly wasn't dressed for the jungle. Unknown jungles were dangerous, even with all the right equipment—and she had neither machete nor bug nets to protect her, let alone a contingency plan for crossing paths with any large predators.

With that thought in mind, she looked both ways down the beach. One choice was as good as the other, but if she made it to the cliffs she saw a good distance down the coastline to her left, she would have more shade, and maybe a cave for shelter.

She stood and began to walk in that direction, but caught herself before she went too far. She wondered, *If Amon comes after me and I'm not here, how will he know where to look for me?*

She got down on her knees in the sand, made sure she was far enough back from the surf that not even a very high tide would reach her. She cupped her fingers and dragged her hands through the sand like she was building a moat around a sandcastle. Instead of a moat, she spelled out Amon's name in letters three feet tall. To the right of his name, she carved a big arrow pointing toward the cliffs, her target destination.

She walked to the water and looked back, making sure it was legible. She could read it from several feet away.

As a last measure, she retrieved a couple big sticks from the dense jungle and pressed them deep into the sand so they stood straight up, marking the place.

That would have to do. It was as big a signpost as she could make on short notice. Barring an extremely high tide, gale-force winds, or a heavy rainstorm, she had carved his name deep enough in the sand to last for several days.

That was good. The last thing she wanted was for him to show up, not find her, and then leave without her.

Satisfied with her work, she turned from it and set a course toward the cliffs.

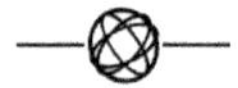

A mile was an optimistic estimate, Eliana thought as she trudged through damp sand. She simply misjudged the sheer size of the cliffs, and therefore the distance to approach. The enormous pale walls of rock reflected a piercing glare from which Eliana had to shield her eyes with one hand until her head stopped throbbing.

She must have been out of shape or something. The muscles in her legs ached, and it was all she could do to put one foot in front of the other. Walking down by the water in the wet, firm sand proved to be easier—both on her weary body and on the bare pink skin of her feet. The sea was the temperature of bathwater, but it only provided a modicum of cooling relief.

As for the beach itself, there wasn't so much as a piece of trash in the sand. This only served to reinforce the idea that wherever she'd been sent, it wasn't Earth. People would have littered this beautiful length of virgin coast with empty bottles, food wrappers, and copious cigarette butts decades ago if this was the planet she knew as home. Here, one detected almost no sign of human life at all. Only the occasional piece of driftwood—at once a happy and a miserable observation.

Eliana rubbed her raw throat. She took a moment to sample the ocean water, but it was salty enough to make her gag and neither quenched her thirst nor replaced the fluids spilling from her pores. The sun shimmered closer to the cliffs as she journeyed toward the shelter they promised. The two moons disappeared from sight as the sun began to fall behind the cliffs.

She couldn't make sense of why she felt so tired. She'd run a marathon once. She'd also worked twelve-hour days at dig sites in desert climates. What she felt was nothing like that. Her exhaustion went all the way to the core of her being.

Twice she had to take a break from walking and sink to her knees in the sand while the world stopped spinning. Each time, she somehow managed to rise again and power on. The thought of Amon kept her going. And the thought of the cool sand at the base of those shady cliffs.

Her new ring, the color of a dark, starry night, served as a constant reminder of Amon. Of course, she couldn't drink the stupid ring.

Step by step, the cliffs drew closer.

Finally, the pale wall of rock loomed overhead, and she stepped into its shadow.

She gasped and fell down, rolling to her back in the cool sand. She pressed her cheek against the ground and inhaled deep, quenching gulps of air.

She pushed herself up and sat with her back to the wall as her eyes adjusted to the shade. She gazed left, letting her head rest against the white rock. Where the cliff made a corner, the beach tapered back and gave way to rocky outcroppings. And something moved around on the rocks.

She rubbed her eyes. Two figures—one cut tall and lean, broad in the chest; the other short and plump, probably female, judging from the proportions. Two people!

In that moment, Eliana didn't care how or why other people had come to reside on this strange planet. She simply took solace in the fact that she wasn't alone on this forsaken stretch of coastline.

Reinvigorated by the prospect of finding help—and the hope that one of them had fresh water—Eliana tapped into a final bastion of strength somewhere deep within her bones, struggled to her feet, and staggered along the cliff wall toward them.

At first, they didn't notice her. The tall figure faced the water and made throwing motions out to sea, his arms swinging over his head in long, slow circles, his fingers wrapped around a fine line. The other bent over something in her lap as she worked it with her hands.

When she got closer, Eliana noticed that the taller figure was bare-chested, a loincloth wrapped around his waist. The woman was dressed much the same.

Within speaking distance, Eliana's heartbeat quickened, and she forgot to speak when she saw that their clothes appeared to be hand-woven, made from a coarse fabric, probably hemp or some kind of cotton.

She stared, dumbstruck. She traced with her mind the intricate, interlocking tattoos carved across the woman's arms and shoulders. She took mental notes about the large, polished pieces of jade hanging from her small earlobes and the experienced handiwork that might craft a necklace of turquoise and seashells like the one dangling from her neck.

Eliana's eyes widened and she tried to say something, to capture her amazement at the sight with words—but her attempt at speech came out as a croak, and the figures spun, startled to notice her for the first time.

Now that their faces were clear, Eliana could see that the woman was old enough to be her mother, but the man was actually a teenager, a boy no more than sixteen or seventeen years old—almost young enough to be her son. His large frame made him seem older from a distance. His shallow chest would one day be deep and strong, his arms thick and brawny, but he had a lot of filling out yet to do. Unlike the woman, he had no tattoos. Perhaps the woman's tattoos had a certain meaning or represented a milestone in life the boy hadn't yet reached. Or perhaps it was a gender distinction. Did she know any society among the ancient civilizations of Earth in which only the women tattooed themselves? The boy did wear a band of stones around one bicep and colorful beads tied into his hair. Both of his forearms were striped with lines of pale scar tissue.

The woman cried out in a guttural language Eliana couldn't place, and at the same time, she felt a light tugging at the hem of her dress. She looked down into the face of a boy, naked and decorated only by a small bone earring poking through the lobe of one ear. He worked the synthetic fabric of Eliana's dress with his fingers, giggling.

The young man reached out and gently pulled the child away from Eliana, placing himself protectively between them.

She thought, *Did I do something wrong? Why are they looking at me like that?*

She worked her dry throat and wiped her hand across her damp forehead. "Water," she managed to say. She blinked to clear the sweat stinging her eyes and lost her balance. She tumbled to the ground, her head bashing against the wall. The blow only registered as relief that she didn't have to hold herself up any longer.

The young man hovered over her as mirror images. He cast twin shadows that spun, identical siblings dancing close and apart, close and then apart.

He looked deeply concerned. His lips moved, but no words came out. His wide, flat forehead wrinkled in the middle when he frowned.

The world moved in slow motion. The sound of waves like echoing footsteps carried her away from her own body, and then darkness took her.

4
SCOURING THE STARS

"REUBEN," AMON CALLED across the stage, forcing his feet to move. "Spin it up again."

Amon wasted no time. He vaulted off the stage to where they'd stashed emergency equipment while Reuben reactivated the displays. The crowd was several dozen yards back, having abandoned their chairs and retreated as far as they could make it in the frantic moments after it had become apparent that something had gone terribly wrong. A few intrepid cameramen saw him and ventured forth, but Amon tossed the spacesuit up onto the stage and climbed up before they got too close. As he stepped into the spacesuit, a familiar whine cut the air. Amon had heard that noise a thousand times before; never had it sounded so ominous.

Lucas mounted the other end of the stage, crossing his arms and swinging them out to his sides.

It was only when he got closer that Amon realized Lucas was talking to him. "No," he was saying. "What are you doing? Are you out of your fucking mind?"

Amon ignored him, turning on the oxygen tank. He fitted the helmet over his head and sealed it. There was no time to talk.

Inside the suit, all Amon could hear was his own labored breathing. Reuben gave him a thumbs-up. To Lucas's arm-waving dismay, Amon strode up the slight incline and stood on the platform in the center of the sphere of rings. He gave Reuben the thumbs-up back, felt a slight lurch in his gut, and a moment later he was in the research dome on the lunar surface.

A pockmarked floor of gray dust stretched out in all directions. Right on target. He cast about for Eliana.

She was nowhere in sight. He stopped breathing.

"Where's the rover?" someone asked.

The voice came in through the comms unit in his helmet from one of three engineers standing in front of him. He couldn't tell which one spoke, but he knew they had come from the Lunar Base in the primary biodome, and that they were expecting the lunar rover.

He did not possess the will to respond. He sank in low-gravity slow motion to the floor, causing a cloud of eons-old dust to billow up around his knees.

After the engineers picked him up, he pushed them away and paced angrily in the lower gravity, clenching his gloved fists and cussing at himself while he waited for Reuben to bring him home. The characteristic high-pitched noise the arch made only sounded Earth-side, so Amon had to ask over the radio whether Reuben had booted the Translocator up again or not. Reuben responded in the affirmative, but he seemed distracted by the chaos of the event.

Amon refused to let his fear for Eliana overwhelm him. He treated it like any problem at the company or with his engineering projects: he pinned it down with a fierce conviction and attacked it.

Trouble was, he didn't know what to attack. He smacked his helmet with a fist. *Think, dammit!*

First of all, he had to believe Eliana was alive. He categorically *refused* to accept the worst-case scenario. But his wife was nowhere in sight, and only time in his lab spent analyzing the faulty translocation would yield any clues to her whereabouts or... anything else.

He walked in circles, ignoring sidelong glances from the surface team while he considered the possibilities and variables in play.

It could have been anything. A loose screw, a bad fitting. The smallest error in a complicated machine had the potential to set off a fatal chain reaction. Picture the faulty o-ring that doomed the space shuttle *Challenger* to explode shortly after takeoff. With a machine as complex as the Hopper, it could take weeks to deconstruct the problem and come to any real conclusions—or solutions.

He already felt the relentless pressure of the ticking clock, so he listed off possibilities. The culprit could be improperly calculated destination coordinates, an erratic spike in energy from the particle accelerator, a flaw in the stabilizing arch, a chink in the alloy spheres.

But that didn't make sense. The blasted thing had sparked like a Tesla coil when Eliana turned it on. Yet it had made a smooth run immediately before and after—one for the rover and one to send Amon himself to the lunar surface.

Those runs went fine. So what had gone wrong with Eliana's? His memory wound back to the moment she had touched the screen, turning at just the right angle to smile at the camera, her fingerprints flattened against the glass. Before the diagnostics started careening off course, her fingers had been zapped by an electric shock—she told him that.

But then everything had happened so fast. He dropped his head, crushed. He paced to keep a surge of rage from building up.

Could it have been the ring, the black diamond known as a carbonado? He dismissed the idea immediately. Diamonds are extremely efficient thermal conductors, but they're electrical *insulators*—meaning they dampen electrical energy, not enhance it. In other words, a diamond couldn't have caused the excess energy Amon saw leaping from nodes on the arch.

He slammed his fist into his helmet on the other side. He needed to see the diagnostics before he could jump to any conclusions. And to do that, he needed to be back on Earth.

"What the hell is taking so long?" he yelled into his helmet. No one responded. "I've been up here for fucking ages!"

"Sorry, just a minute," Reuben said. "There's a bit of a scene down here."

"Bring me back."

"Uhh..."

"Do it!"

The Hopper could only be activated from one end. No magnificent arch or high-tech displays needed to be constructed on the lunar surface. Only a blue-green platform mounted in the ground, recognizable because it was marked with a Fisk Industries sigil, which projected a magnetic field and transmitted coordinates to the machine on Earth.

Looking down at the bold sans-serif *FI* engraved in the alloy, Amon thought how arrogant it had been to put his name on the moon like that. It had seemed like a declaration of something important when he'd sent the design to the Lunar Station to have them 3-D print and set it. Now, the dust-blown letters silently mocked his folly.

The platform's material glowed softly.

"Finally," Amon said. He walked onto the platform without preamble. His stomach lurched at the familiar disorientation, and he found himself back on Earth.

Pulling off his helmet, he stepped from the sphere into a buzzing throng of reporters.

Lost in his thoughts, they took him by surprise—the camera lenses, the digital recorders, the handheld devices and booms and mics, all shoved into his face, sucking away the very air. The cold ball of iron in his gut shot off, tearing the tenuous walls of self-control he had established with his logical analysis mere moments before.

"Mr. Fisk, what went wrong tonight?"

"Is your wife alive?" Pops, flashes, microphones shoved in his face.

"Is molecular reassembly truly a safe technology after what we just witnessed?"

"I..." Amon said. "Um."

Amon stammered for a moment, acutely aware of the cameras, before Lucas swooped in to replace him with Fisk Industries' media liaison, a tall, confident brunette with thick-rimmed glasses.

"I'm sorry," she said, "Mr. Fisk won't be taking any questions at this time. Thank you for coming. We'll release a statement first thing tomorrow."

Grateful he didn't have to tell the lies himself, Amon let Reuben and Lucas place their arms over his shoulders and lead him inside.

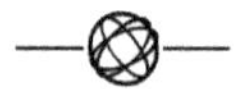

In the vast underground lab beneath the campus's quad where the Hopper was kept, Reuben helped Amon out of the bulky spacesuit while the rest of the project team lowered the massive machine down into the lab and began to run diagnostic tests.

Lucas took phone calls from the internal teleconference line wired into one of the lab's computers for a while, reassuring the board of directors, various departments within the company, and the heads of several government agencies that everything was under control. But he kept bumping into people while they were trying to work, and eventually he pulled out his cell phone and went upstairs where the signal was stronger.

"The director of the FBI is calling already? Christ!" Lucas said into the phone as he left the lab. "Fine, fine, put him through."

Reuben barked one-word orders at the project team, a selection of the brightest engineering and scientific minds of a generation: four biologists, two biochemists, six astrophysicists, eight engineers, and Reuben, plus Amon himself. Amon dabbled in a little bit of everything, but he knew the depth of experience that came from his team, and he trusted them to do their work faster and better than he could on his own. Reuben, the gruff old sergeant, knew their strengths and weaknesses, how to be demanding and forgiving at all the right times in order to bring out the best in them.

Someone brought Amon a cup of tea. He sat in his wrinkled tux with the shirt untucked as the mug grew cold in his hands. When the reports had been generated, they laid out the data in rows on the tables, which doubled as digital surfaces, and in navigable gesture-controlled arrays on screens embedded into two walls of the room.

His team pored over them, comparing notes and rehashing every moment of each translocation earlier that evening. They regrouped to discuss the occasional clarifying question: How did everyone interpret this energy spike here? Could it have occurred at the moment Eliana's finger came into contact with the display screen? Could her high adrenaline level have had an effect on the disassembly process? They prowled the territory in crisscrossing patterns, scouring it for a clue that would point them in the right direction.

When they'd circled around it enough, and Amon finally came to accept that they might as well be tracking down a needle in a haystack—or rather, a single needle in a whole field of haystacks—he called a pause to the hunt.

"Go home to your families," he said. "Rest. We'll regroup in the morning."

"It's 5:30 a.m.," Reuben said.

"Is it?"

The scientists left one by one, patting him on the shoulder. Jeanine, a biochemist, gave him a hug.

"I'll be back in two hours," said Walter, an astrophysicist. "We'll find her, boss."

Amon nodded and forced a smile. When everyone but Reuben was gone, he ran to the nearest trashcan and dry heaved into it. When that passed, he sank against the wall and closed his throbbing eyes.

The search continued nonstop for two weeks while Lucas desperately maneuvered to keep the media and the government agencies at bay. In the end, the exact destination of Eliana's reassembly remained unclear. In layman's terms, the angle and direction of her translocation was obvious, but she'd somehow overshot the mark. They couldn't make heads or tails of where she ended up, at least not to an exact degree because of the enormous distance she seemed to have covered. They did manage to narrow down her vector to a small patch of sky, a tiny sampling of space that contained millions of stars. But this area hadn't been extensively mapped by the Kepler Observatory, and to gather that data would take time.

"Where is she, Reuben?" Amon asked one night when they were the only two left in the lab.

"Somewhere in that section of sky."

"That could be fucking anywhere. How are we supposed to find her?"

Reuben pursed his lips but remained silent.

"And that's assuming she even reassembled at all," Amon went on, breathing heavy. "What if she's just dust motes floating through space forever? What if she materialized in the middle of nowhere and froze to death?"

Reuben's frown deepened. "Don't say that."

"You and I both know that's the *far* more likely scenario. She either exploded in the vacuum, her blood boiling and freezing at the same time—"

"Stop," Reuben said between his teeth.

"—or she never reassembled at all."

"Amon..."

Amon lumbered to his feet as he raised his voice. "Her body was torn into a million little pieces and is doomed to wander the vast nothingness—"

Amon's face exploded in pain as Reuben's fist sailed into his jaw. Amon stared at his friend, stunned.

"I didn't want to do that," Reuben said, "but you need to keep your head on straight."

Seething, Amon swallowed blood from a cut on his tongue.

"It's the beginning of the end when you start talking like that." Reuben turned away, shaking his hand out.

It had been a trying two weeks for everyone, but it occurred to Amon that Reuben wasn't necessarily talking about Eliana, at least not entirely, and his anger fizzled out. Reuben didn't like to speak of it, but Amon knew he had put his partner of thirty years in a nursing home last year.

"Early onset Alzheimer's," Reuben had said simply after closing the door to Amon's office and sitting on the edge of a chair one day.

"I'm so sorry," Amon had said, and meant it. "Anything you need."

That had been the end of the conversation, but Amon saw how Reuben spent more time at the lab in recent months, how the skin under his eyes bruised from lack of sleep, and how he kept checking his phone at work. If anyone knew what Amon was going through right now, what it meant to lose a life partner, it was Reuben.

"I'm sorry," Amon said, rubbing his jaw. "Damn, you throw a mean right hook."

Reuben smirked. "And you thought I was an old *putz*."

"Never."

A moment of silence passed.

"Don't you want to go home?" Amon asked.

"I'd rather not."

"Me either."

Reuben slept on the couch in the lounge beside the kitchenette. Amon gave up trying. Instead, he quieted his mind by keeping his hands busy and tinkered with one of two mobile transponder prototypes he and Reuben had begun testing immediately after the accident.

Amon would need to carry the transponder with him when he went through after Eliana, since wherever she ended up didn't have a transponder embedded in the ground like they had at the Lunar Station. The prototype they had thrown together was clunky, the size of an old TV remote, and not even close to functional. Nonetheless, the motions of taking it apart, systematically lining all the pieces up, and then putting it back together again calmed him. It wasn't sleep, but it worked as a kind of meditation.

When Reuben woke, he suggested some vitamin D therapy, so they made their way above ground to the café on campus. They sat watching the sun rise through a cool dawn while they ate freshly toasted bagels and sipped hot coffee.

The campus began to teem with FI employees arriving for work. Instead of returning to the laboratory with Reuben, Amon walked across the quad. Those he passed avoided meeting his eyes. By now, they all knew the story, and his insane hours were often discussed. Those who had been paying attention to murmurings among the executive team also knew that the board of directors had called an all-hands meeting for this morning, and Amon had no choice but to attend.

5
HEALER, SHAMAN, CHIEF

A BRIEF FLASH OF light startled Eliana awake. She panicked, casting about for something to grab onto. She came up with handfuls of dried grass, her fingernails scraping stone beneath her.

The light expanded then shrank back to a sliver, disappearing as a heavy door inched shut. She tried to sit up, but the knotted muscles in her neck prevented her from rising.

A woman kneeled by her side, the same short, shapely woman she'd approached on the beach. It was difficult to make out her features in the dim light, but Eliana recognized the turquoise-and-seashell necklace and the polished ovals of her jade earrings.

She struggled to lift herself to her elbows, but the woman put one hand on her chest and pressed her back down, holding a clay mug filled with a warm liquid to Eliana's lips.

The acrid concoction gave off a bitter licorice smell with faint undertones of citrus. Eliana struggled, wrinkling her nose and turning away, her cramped neck muscles twitching. But the woman held the back of Eliana's head with the other hand and forced her to drink. Much of the liquid dribbled down her chin, but some made it into her mouth, quenching her thirst and soothing her raw throat.

The woman placed the empty cup on the floor and built a small fire with the dry grass while Eliana caught her breath.

Eliana watched with fascination, wiping the sweat from her feverish brow, as the old lady fed handfuls of something from a dried gourd—likely incense and herbs, Eliana guessed—into the flames.

As she watched, her eyelids began to droop of their own accord. Whether she was exhausted from the journey to this strange planet, or there had been a sedative mixed into the bitter drink the medicine woman had force fed her, Eliana didn't know. But the woman didn't seem to wish her harm.

She turned her neck straight to ease the pain from her cramped muscles. While the room filled with smoke, she fell back into unconsciousness.

She dreamed that she had found her way back to the pristine white beach somehow. Amon's name had been washed out by the waves, and she recognized her location only by the two sticks standing several feet apart like a gateway to nowhere.

Looking through the gateway, a path opened up into the jungle, a wide road leading into the trees, paved with white stones.

Curious, Eliana followed it. After she'd gone a few yards, the paving stones began to crack and crumble. They soon gave way to a dirt trail, and when she looked back, the trees had closed in over top of the trail as if it had never existed.

When she looked forward again, the dirt trail was gone, too. The forest had crowded in around her so that she was wading through a sea of dense green-and-purple foliage with bright orange-and-blue flowers.

The sun winked out like God had flipped a switch controlling the heavens. A low growl rumbled from somewhere beneath the impenetrable surface of leaves that coated the jungle floor and buried Eliana to mid-thigh, and two discs opened in the dark sky, bathing the sea of flora in silvery moonlight—the two moons hidden behind the canopy.

A pair of red glowing eyes dodged around a tree at the edge of the clearing and bobbed through the brush, headed straight for her.

She booked it in the other direction, arms pumping, back the way she'd come through thick brush, branches smacking her in the face and leaving long scratches.

The creature yowled into the night as it stalked her. Eliana knew she was not faster than a jungle cat, but she seemed to be staying ahead of it nonetheless, as if the creature maintained that distance for the fun of the chase. Frightened, Eliana ran on.

Without warning, the tree line ended, and the ground dropped out beneath her. Eliana pulled up, falling to the ground and skidding, her feet extending over the edge of a sheer cliff. Sharp breakers jutted out from the cliff wall into a violently crashing indigo ocean hundreds of feet below. Birds circled beneath her.

Two moons hung in the sky above the sparkling sea. The bigger of the two was missing a significant portion of the upper right quadrant, as if it had been bitten off by a giant set of gnashers. Its jagged edge dripped. It was bleeding.

Eliana spun, staring into the red gemstone eyes of an oversized jaguar. Her hands scrabbled back over the edge of the cliff, desperately seeking purchase but finding only air.

The jaguar licked its lips.

Eliana jumped up, panting, and retreated into a cold corner. She shivered and wrapped her thin body in her goose-flesh-covered arms.

As her breathing returned to normal and the terror that crossed the bridge of consciousness from her dream subsided, Eliana inspected the room she occupied. Instead of the thick foliage of a dense jungle, four bare limestone walls surrounded her, and a wooden slat door barred the only exit. Eliana put a finger into the pile of cold ashes where the woman had burned the incense. She had no concept how long ago she had last awoken, but the air had cleared. The clay mug sat on the floor where it had been left.

Eliana took a mental inventory of herself. She still wore her black cocktail dress, but apart from a dry throat and cracked lips her mind felt clear and more lucid than it had since the demonstration. Sweat dripped down her brow, but that seemed to be a natural effect of the tropical environment rather than the cold fever-sweats she experienced before.

The bitter taste of the concoction the woman fed her lingered in her mouth. Upon inspecting the clay mug, Eliana found it filled with a translucent liquid that smelled faintly of sulfur. She sipped it cautiously, and it had no taste except the minerals, like unfiltered spring water. She paused to wonder if the water had a lavender tint, but she couldn't tell in the dim room. Some light filtered in around the edges of the wooden door, but there were no windows, no candles, no torches—certainly no sign of electricity.

Screw it, she thought. She gulped the water down and sighed as it quenched her still-raw throat.

Eliana stood, arching her arms overhead, slowly pulling out the soreness in her muscles by gripping one wrist with the other hand and leaning to each side in turn. She counted in her head as she pulled in long, slow breaths of thick air through her nose.

After stretching, she paced around the room while she eyeballed the door. Testing it, she found it locked but forced herself to stay calm. Maybe they locked the door to keep her safe from whatever beasts stalked in the jungle. Or maybe it was simply to protect themselves from her. She was a stranger here, after all—better safe than sorry.

Voices carried through the door, but they subsided. A short time later, a shuffling noise announced movement outside. The door cracked open, and a woman entered, closing the door behind her.

Eliana retreated, bowing her head. She wasn't sure how to look at the woman before her. Some cultures found a direct gaze to be an insult or a threat. She certainly did not want to insult her benefactor, but she couldn't help making a quick study of the shapely figure. Apart from her normal jewelry, she wore a beige hand-woven dress that extended to her knees and flowed loosely. She also wore wooden sandals, which Eliana immediately envied. If she was ever to leave the room, she'd need some kind of practical shoes.

The woman picked up the clay mug and checked that it had been emptied. Reaching out, she gripped Eliana's chin in one strong hand and gazed deep into her eyes. Apparently satisfied with what she saw, the woman grunted and let her go. Then she sat on the straw and patted the floor, inviting Eliana to sit down.

"*Bix a k'aaba*?" she said after Eliana had crossed her legs beneath her.

Eliana cocked her head. She was no linguist, but foreign tongues had always come easy to her. Apart from German, she had a passing familiarity with Spanish and a smattering of Mayan she'd gathered on research trips to Guatemala and Belize. The words the woman spoke sounded strikingly similar to a variety of ancient Mesoamerican dialects, perhaps distantly related to the language of the Maya, Olmec, or Zoque peoples.

Eliana shook her head. "I'm sorry, but I don't understand you."

"*Ixchel in k'aaba*," the woman said, steepling her fingers against her own chest, then poking Eliana with one finger. "*Bix a k'aaba*?"

A gear turned in Eliana's mind, and she gasped. "Eliana," she said. "My name is Eliana."

"*Eliana in k'aaba,*" the woman said. This time Eliana made out the hard glottal stop after the k and separated the word with an apostrophe in her mind.

"*Eliana in k'aaba,*" she said, butchering the pronunciation.

The woman nodded, satisfied. She mouthed Eliana's name a few more times then made Eliana repeat her own name until she got the pronunciation right: Ixchel, pronounced eesh-chel, like the second half of sheesh and the first half of cello.

An old memory flooded to the surface of Eliana's mind from a class on ancient religions of Mesoamerican peoples, which she'd audited in grad school. She remembered the professor going through the pantheon of Mayan gods—they had hundreds of gods, thousands by some accounts. Ixchel, however, she remembered: it was the name of the goddess of childbirth and medicine.

A deep voice bellowed outside. Ixchel started, and they both scrambled to their feet. The voice sounded again, closer this time, and the door swung open.

A large figure appeared in the door frame. Ixchel rushed to the door as he squeezed his broad shoulders into the room. Her eyes adjusted slowly to the light pouring in around the man's large frame. Every inch of his barrel chest and thick arms were covered with intricate tattoos. She corrected an earlier assumption: women and men both tattooed themselves.

The man also sported elaborate shoulder pauldrons made of bone and wood. The bits of bone were carved with skulls, which grinned in neat little rows. A bone through the septum of his nose gave him a hungry expression like an enraged bull.

He spoke to Ixchel in the guttural tongue—it seemed like he was berating her, but perhaps that was simply Eliana's interpretation of the harsh, unfamiliar sound of the language. In any case, Ixchel seemed unperturbed. She pushed past him and left then returned a moment later with a new clay mug of water to replace the old one.

Without another glance, they both left the room and closed the door behind them.

Eliana heard the bolt slide back into place. She crept to the door and gazed through the crack around the edges into the daylight.

Ixchel was nowhere to be seen. The big man's broad back took up most of her view. He spoke, presumably to other people Eliana couldn't see. Another man approached behind him, this one older and more elaborately clothed, with a great feathered headdress and plenty of jewelry—gems, stones, and bones—knocking together around his arms, wrists, and ankles. A long, white cloth was draped across his shoulders. Eliana could only guess, but based on his clothing he must have been some kind of shaman or priest.

He spoke in a loud, intoning voice—overly theatrical, Eliana thought. The big man turned to face him and took the tongue lashing. His fists clenched and unclenched while he waited. When the shaman had stopped yelling, the big man said a few clipped words. The shaman responded by pointing at the sky with a finger then past the big man at the door behind which Eliana hid.

The big man turned and pointed a finger at the door, too. He said a few words to whoever was standing out of view on either side then walked away.

Someone's face loomed into Eliana's vision and peered through at her. She threw herself back and scurried into the far corner. When she worked up the courage to return to the door and gaze out again, everyone seemed to have gone. She saw trees and leaves, and heard the buzz of insects and breathed the dense air.

With shaking hands, she picked up the new clay mug of water and downed that, too.

A short time later, as Eliana sat in the darkness, her heart began to beat faster. Her throat went dry, and a sheet of metal lined her stomach.

She clung tightly to her knees and rocked back and forth as the walls began to drip indigo like the broken moon in her nightmare.

6
UNKNOWN AGENTS

AMON BOUNDED UP the steps and pulled open the heavy front door of a Gothic building that housed their corporate offices.

Lucas waited for him in the lobby. He matched Amon's stride, and together they climbed the wooden stairs to the boardroom on the top floor.

"What's their mood like?" Amon asked.

"Dour. What happened to your nose?"

"Shit," Amon said, stopping on a landing between flights of stairs.

Lucas withdrew a handkerchief from the breast pocket of his suit, which Amon used to wipe away the dried blood around his nostrils.

Lucas waited patiently. As usual, his suit was immaculately pressed. Amon looked down at his own rumpled attire, and swore when he realized he'd forgotten to change clothes as well. There was no time to go back for the change of clothes he kept in the lab, so he turned and continued up the stairs, breathing though his nose to get a handle on the frustration he felt.

"Do you really think they're bluffing?" Lucas asked.

"We'll know soon enough."

Amon threw open the door to the boardroom. To his irritation, Wes McManis had started without them and was currently delivering a soliloquy to the assembled directors with his usual snake-oil salesman demeanor. Amon had to admit, allowing a sonofabitch like Wes to be appointed to the board had been useful at times. McManis had political and business connections that had been a boon for the company. He was loaded, too. But it was a damned clumsy mistake. Not for the first time, Amon wished he'd been less ambitious in his youth. His impatience to get ahead had caused him more than a few headaches over the years.

"What our company needs," Wes was saying, "is strong leadership in this moment of crisis."

"I couldn't agree more," Amon said from the doorway.

"Ah," Wes gestured expansively. "Hello, Amon. Glad you could make it." Amon saw the ripple effect of his withering tone on the faces of the assembled board members. They seemed either amused or mildly irritated but didn't call Wes's flippant attitude into question.

"Thanks for getting started," Amon said. "I think I can take it from here." Most of the assembled directors avoided his gaze. He supposed this estrangement was how people who were grieving must feel in a crowded room—isolated, nervous, worried. He clenched his jaw, refusing to give in to the flood of emotions. He forced himself to stay calm and rational.

"The search continues," Amon said. "We're getting close to finding Eliana."

Wes grimaced, not even trying to hide his contempt. "You have my deepest condolences, Amon," Wes said.

"But is that really true?" At least he had the balls to say what was on everyone else's mind.

"We're just getting started," Amon insisted. "The Translocator team has been running diagnostic tests and simulations, piecing Eliana's jump together. We haven't narrowed down her exact coordinates, but we've tracked her vector, and we're confident we'll locate her very soon."

A few heads perked up. Amon glanced over to see Wes silently taking a poll of the room's opinion.

"Of course," Wes said, switching gears. "That's great news. Every second counts... which is even more reason to give you some time off. So you can focus on finding your poor wife."

"What do you mean?" he said, his fingers involuntarily curling into fists.

"I'm suggesting that you step down from your post as CEO, of course."

What was astonishing was not Wes's suggestion—that was to be expected, and Amon had fallen for the trick. What was amazing was that Amon couldn't argue the logic of it. Taking some time off would be the smart thing to do, the responsible decision made in the best interests of the company. Despite the confidence he hoped he exuded, the thought of Eliana consumed him even now. Standing in this room, arguing with Wes, seemed like an incredible waste of time. Eliana was more important than the approval of the board, more important than the Lunar Station, more important than his company and everything he'd worked his whole life to build. She *was* his life.

And yet if he couldn't protect the Translocator from the Wes McManises of the world, he'd never be able to find Eliana.

"Lucas could take over as interim CEO during the transition," Wes suggested.

Amon pursed his lips. He could never trust the company to Wes, even with Lucas at the helm. If Wes managed to remove him as CEO of the company, he would have no power to protect the Translocator. Amon had no choice but to dig his heels in now. For Eliana.

"No," Amon said, turning from Wes's weasel face to look at the seated members of the board. "Lucas will continue in his current position, of course, and I'm more than grateful for the support from each of you in this trying time. But I'm not taking a leave of absence."

"Amon, please—" Wes began.

"This is a temporary situation."

"It won't look good," said Miguel Ortiz, an old Mexican who had made his fortune shipping avocados into the United States. He'd been on the board of directors since the company's infancy. "Wes is right. We need to show that we have the situation under control. Our investors will be worried if you don't take a leave of absence, given the current situation."

"Showing our investors that we support Amon is all that matters," Lucas said.

"And who will be there to support you when Amon is...preoccupied?" Ortiz asked, intertwining the fingers of both hands. A gold ring on his pinky caught the morning light that slanted in through the windows.

Amon felt his eyes widen, his nostrils flare and pull in air. When a phone rang and Lucas stepped from the room to take the call, Amon barely noticed.

"Amon?" he heard Miguel say.

Amon snapped his jaw closed. It was important to appear strong now. "Miguel, you're right. And thank you for being honest with me. You've been a reliable and generous friend since the very beginning, and I appreciate your support. Whoever is leading this company, we need to present a united front. I'll have no more division among the board. We'll take a vote, and whatever the outcome, I'll abide by it. If you vote to remove me, I'll resign today."

Appealing to Ortiz's loyalty and sticking to his guns had precisely the effect Amon had hoped for. He saw the old man's brow line relax, his posture soften.

Wes crossed his arms. "Fine," he said. "All who would like Amon to stay on as CEO, raise your hand."

Amon raised his hand, never taking his gaze from Ortiz's face. Slowly, the old Mexican raised his hand as well, followed by one, then three, then five more hands. Amon took a quick mental tally. With his 40 percent of the company, plus Ortiz's faction voting with him, they made a majority.

"There," Amon said, watching a snarl of rage form on Wes's face as he did the math for himself. "It's settled."

He forgot to thank them all for coming, but that didn't register until later. Amon pulled his phone from his pocket as he left the room and with shaky fingers dialed Reuben in the lab to share his wild theory.

On his way to the lab, Lucas intercepted him. A man and a woman in dark suits followed in his wake. They each wore Fisk Industries guest passes on their lapels. The man wore glasses and had thin lips arranged in what seemed to be a permanent scowl. The woman's hair was cropped short, almost military, and she carried a heavy duty file folder in her hands.

"Mr. Fisk?" the woman said, holding out a stiff hand.

"Yes?" Amon took her hand, felt her cool dry fingers in contrast to his own sweaty palms.

"May we speak in private?"

Reuben, anticipating Amon's arrival, turned the corner a moment later. Before Amon could say anything else, Lucas spoke. "Reuben, would you mind showing our guests to the conference room please?"

Reuben nodded, exchanged a glance with Amon, and led the two away.

"We have a problem," Lucas whispered.

"I don't have time for this right now."

"I held them off as long as I could, but it's out of my control now."

Taking a deep breath, Amon followed them into the conference room. The woman spoke before he got the door closed. "I'm sorry for your loss, Mr. Fisk."

Amon closed the door. "What do you mean?"

She blinked, saying nothing. The other man piped up instead, his voice rising to a nervous pitch. "For the death of your wife, Mr. Fisk."

"Eliana is alive and well," Amon said. He managed to hold a smile while he swallowed the lump in his throat. After years of working on cutting-edge solar energy transformers and particle physics experiments, Amon knew that exuding confidence in the end result you desired was most vital when the outcome appeared bleak. That kind of brass-balls attitude had pulled him across the finish line more often than dumb luck or clever engineering ever had.

"Ah…" the man stammered.

"Please, sit down," Amon said, gesturing vaguely to the chairs arranged around a long table as he eased himself into a seat. "How can I help you?"

"I'm sure you've got a lot on your mind," the woman went on as she sat. "That's why I'm hoping we can work together."

"Who's 'we'?"

"I'm Libby Fowler, and this is George Montoya."

"I mean, who do you work for, Miss Fowler?"

"The Federal Bureau of Investigation," she said, pulling out a brass badge with the letters *FBI* stamped over the agency's seal.

"How can I help you?"

"Our department handles… sensitive situations."

"What department is that?"

"Rest assured, I have complete authority in this matter."

"And this matter is what, exactly?"

"I hope we can count on your full cooperation, Mr. Fisk. We've taken the time to draft a statement for you. To give to the press."

His heart did a little pitter-patter at mention of the press. Journalists had continued to phone the company daily since the accident, requesting interviews and statements. He could keep his cool in the lab, but he feared his mask would crumble in front of the cameras. Reuben noticed his discomfort and placed a hand on his shoulder while Fowler reached into her folder and withdrew a piece of paper.

Amon stuffed down the rage that threatened to boil over while he read it. Lucas and Reuben read over his shoulder.

"Bullshit!" Lucas said, slamming his fist down on the table. "Shut down the Auriga Project, are you kidding me?"

Amon held up a hand. "I'll get the LTA Administrator on the phone right now," he said. "There's no way he authorized this."

"I'm afraid he has," Fowler said. "This is a matter of public safety, Mr. Fisk."

"Over a hundred countries contributed funds to the Auriga Project. This is an international effort. The FBI can't just shut it down."

"As you know, the LTA is primarily funded by the United States government. National security is a priority."

"I don't believe it," Lucas grumbled.

Reuben, with his arms crossed, remained stoically silent.

Amon picked up the phone and dialed the number of Dr. Badeux. No answer or answering machine. The line rang and rang. He tried the deputy administrator then on down the line. But after four attempts, he sat back in his chair and met Fowler's level gaze.

"They'll call back," Lucas said.

"Here's what's going to happen, Mr. Fisk." Fowler's smile had vanished. "You're going to give that statement to the press this afternoon. And then you're going to shut down the Auriga Project."

"And if I don't?"

"Then the LTA will withdraw your funding, and you'll be forced to shut down anyway."

"You can't be serious. We've spent ten years and billions of dollars on the program."

"With the death of your wife—"

"She's not dead."

Montoya snorted. Amon noticed a bulge under the right arm of the man's suit.

Reuben pinned him with a look. "Listen, you little..."

"Easy," Amon said.

Fowler interlaced her fingers. "The decision was not mine, but I have the full authority of the FBI and the LTA in this matter."

"I don't believe you," Amon said.

"Your belief is none of my concern."

"I won't give this statement."

"This was a courtesy, Mr. Fisk. I didn't have to come here at all."

"Then get the hell out."

Her cold smile returned. "As you wish," she said, standing. "The Auriga Project will be shut down. It's just a matter of time. You'll see."

She left. Montoya followed her, flipping Reuben off through the glass wall of the conference room.

"Real professional," Reuben said.

"Shit, shit, shit," Lucas mumbled.

"Calm down," Amon said.

"Calm down!?" Lucas's voice rose an octave. "How can you say calm down? I can't believe this is happening."

Amon didn't reply. He knew the feeling. First the board meeting, and now this. Any normal person would have been grateful that Wes had the best interests of the company at heart in the wake of such a tragedy; had it been Amon who had disappeared onstage that night, he'd have been able to rest easy knowing Wes and Lucas were at the helm.

But it wasn't, and he couldn't. And now, on top of the search for Eliana, in spite of the fact that he had barely avoided mutiny at the board meeting, the FBI was manipulating the LTA to shut him down.

It sounded paranoid when he said it out loud, but the only thing that was clear to him was that someone was trying to sabotage his search for Eliana. He had to move faster, to stay ahead of their machinations. So he and Reuben climbed into Reuben's Ford Taurus and left the Fisk Industries campus without telling anyone.

7
THE COLOR OF SACRIFICE

ELIANA LOST HER mind for the next while. Her sense of time distorted. Two days or ten: She couldn't tell. A parade of spirits from her past life came and left, entering and exiting through walls of stone that rippled like the surface of a roiling sea.

Once she figured out the visions were the result of some kind of psychoactive agent she had ingested rather than a forestalled symptom caused by the molecular reassembly process, she managed to relax and let them come rather than fight against the inexorable tide of chemicals that flooded her brain.

From time to time, the door would crack open and food and water would be set down inside her cell, no doubt laced with more of whatever it was they were feeding her. Twice, a chamber pot in the far corner was carried out to be emptied, and returned to its place.

She ate the salted fish and dried fruits and bitter nuts they left because her body demanded fuel. Sweat poured down her skin, and her palms were constantly damp.

At first, she tried to drink as little of the water as possible, knowing it was drugged. But even with a draft from the half-inch gap around the door, the stifling heat of the cell was intolerable. In the end, she always drank the water, and it was fresh and sweet, and she continued to hallucinate.

Elevated to this state, her mind reacted slowly when the door to her cell was thrown wide. The shaman she had seen through the crack in the door entered. A black-and-red band was painted across his eyes and the lower half of his unusually flat, wrinkled forehead. He carried a torch in his ancient hand—a pitch torch the likes of which Eliana had only seen in movies—and held it away from his elaborate feathered headdress.

Two women, barely older than teenagers by contemporary American standards, stepped into the cell from behind him with laden arms. They set pots of water, *incensarios,* and dried gourds on the floor around her.

Eliana didn't realize her visitors and their supplies were more than hallucinations until the two women began to wash her feet with wet rags. The water felt incredible on her skin, so at first she simply reveled in the sensation.

Before she could react, they pulled her dress halfway up her torso. She scrambled away, pulling her dress down and blushing. Their shy smiles flickered in the dancing torchlight, but the shaman snapped an order, and they hurriedly pulled Eliana's dress over her shoulders in spite of her protests.

She covered herself with her hands while the women finished bathing her. Their motions were smooth and practiced, firm but gentle. They did her no harm, and after enough complaining, Eliana dropped her arms and let them work.

The shaman leered at her naked breasts then stepped out of the room.

She breathed easier with him gone and gazed around to take stock of her situation. Through the open door, a sliver of a moon hung low, bright enough to cast the shadows of tree branches onto the ground. The door remained open, like her captors had no intention of closing it again.

Yet the shaman waited outside while the women prepared her for something. It was not unusual for a culture to include bathing as part of a ritual, but if she was being bathed now, what ritual was she about to undergo? She searched for clues. *Incensarios*, big clay mugs thatched with holes to hold incense for spiritual cleansing, lay next to dried gourds filled with purple liquid. Eliana noted the fine craftsmanship of the tools, particularly the coarse brushes whose bristles poked out of a square of cloth.

Something about the purple paint gave Eliana pause, but she couldn't pair it with any particular meaning from her own studies, nor from her memory of research trips she had taken to Mexico, Turkey, Thailand, or one of a myriad of other countries. The work her company had done, while it was still solvent, consisted mostly of repairs and restoration work to minor structures. A few promising leads had come in, like the jawbone fragment they uncovered in Belize but which turned out to belong to a female ape. Maybe things would have turned out differently, she reflected, if she had swallowed her pride and asked Amon for money instead of begging for spare change and odd jobs from the dwindling number of cultural institutions left on Earth.

Her mind wandered, taken again by the drugs, and she forgot what she was looking for. Fingers brushed her thighs as one of the women tried to remove her panties. Eliana yelped and smacked the woman's hand away. The archaeologist in her wanted to provide a justification for the woman's violation, but it didn't seem right. It was one thing to be comfortable with nudity, another to strip someone without permission.

"No," she said. "No freaking way."

The women glanced to the door. The shaman appeared, shrugged, and they let her be.

So she stood wearing nothing but her underwear and Amon's ring. Eliana saw how the women's eyes fixed on the ring. As for how much of their words she understood, she might as well not have been present. In the end, they came to a decision and tied a loincloth around Eliana's waist then fitted her with some plain jewelry pulled from the supplies they brought: a necklace of seashells, a bracelet of stones.

Finally, taking up brushes, they began to apply purple paint to Eliana's skin, starting with her feet.

Her heart beat faster, imagining herself as a piece of meat being basted in some kind of marinade. Could she make it through the door before they caught her if she kicked the young one in the face and made a break for it? She didn't think these people were cannibals, but what kind of outward evidence would one look for? She had seen bones used as decoration, but were they *human* bones?

Maybe they did plan to eat her. Absence of evidence is not evidence of absence, as Amon would say.

The next step after marinating a piece of meat is to lash it to a spit and hang it over a fire.

At that thought, she lost her composure. She jerked away. The women grabbed her, and she fought back with nails and elbows and knees.

While she was trying to wrap her fingers around the long strands of one woman's braids, someone lifted her off her feet.

The shaman's arms gripped Eliana around the midsection while she writhed. His torch had been set down inside the stone room.

"Please," she sobbed, scratching at his forearms. "Let me go!"

The women resumed painting her stomach.

"No," Eliana moaned. "No, no, no."

She whipped her body back and forth and succeeded in taking the old man down.

He rolled on top of her and held her down with a knee across her waist. He was much stronger than he looked. He gripped her wrists over her head with one hand and pressed his other hand down on top of her bare chest.

She froze when the realization hit her. Early in the twentieth century, an explorer named Edward Thompson had dredged the bottom of the Sacred Cenote, a huge rainwater reservoir the Maya associated with the sky god, Chaak. From that well in the famous late city of Chichen Itza, they pulled pottery, pieces of jade, and not a few skeletons. What made the story incredible, however, was not what they pulled out, but what they left in: they discovered that a fourteen-foot layer of blue sediment coated the bottom of the cenote.

Empty blue skies spelled trouble for an ancient people reliant on seasonal rain to grow their food. Thus, the researchers concluded, the Maya used the color blue, in honor of Chaak, to represent sacrifice—they painted the pots and jewels with an azure dye and cast their prayers into the deep.

The color difference was why she'd missed the connection at first. But wasn't it obvious? On this planet, where the sky was a violet hue, the color of sacrifice was purple like the paint drying on her skin.

This thought passed through Eliana's mind in an instant. The women's brushes continued to tickle her shoulders. The shaman pinned her down, his knee crushing her, making it impossible to breathe, and yet she found a reserve of energy within her deep enough to let out a piercing scream that reverberated around the small stone room. Eliana cried for her husband.

"Get off me, you bastards! Amon! AMON!"

He didn't come, and eventually she ran out of breath. Tears blurred her vision when she looked down and saw that her torso, her arms and legs, her hands, even her face was purple.

Voices called out in the jungle. The shaman pulled an obsidian knife from his side and held it to Eliana's throat. He said something then backed off her slowly and stood.

She remained on the ground.

He walked out of the cell, waved to someone out of view, then came back in. He dismissed the women. Picking Eliana up by the elbow, he marched her out the door.

They stepped between two buildings and emerged on a long path of white paving stones. The road had been cracked and tilted by the passage of time, and weeds grew up through the fissures.

The pitch torch had been left in the cell. Exposed beneath the night sky, they didn't need it. Two full moons overhead provided perfect visibility. Not as bright as daylight, but bright enough to see clearly. The large moon was pockmarked like Earth's moon, and was a similar dirty opal in color. It was nearly twice as large as Earth's moon in the night sky. The smaller satellite appeared as a glowing red circle in the inky sky.

A group of men waited for them. The big man she recognized immediately. He was the one who had come into her cell with Ixchel before. The tallest of anyone there, his broad shoulders were draped with skull-carved shoulder pauldrons. Seeing his bearing and dress compared to the other men—who, while painted, showed more skin and were less elaborately costumed—convinced her that he was the chief.

The only one decorated more elaborately than the chief was the shaman.

After gazing at the painted faces of the other men, all younger, she recognized the older of the two boys from the beach. He stood at the chief's right shoulder and looked exactly like a younger version of the big man: same square cleft chin, same prominent nose, same copper skin. Perhaps it was the drugs, but she saw clearly how one day the boy's chest and arms would fill out to match his father's.

From the jungle surrounding them, a deep humming like a low-powered engine began to vibrate. She shook her head, trying to dislodge the noise, but it only increased in volume.

The chief held his hand out toward Eliana and beckoned. The shaman pulled her forward.

Eliana blinked, and a new figure, dressed in black from head to foot, appeared between them. He said something, one garbled, metallic string of words that echoed off the stone walls and mingled with the humming noise.

The chief argued, slicing his hand down through the air.

The shaman halted his forward motion. He glanced sidelong at the dark figure then at the ground while he waited obediently for the argument with the chief to be resolved. While the shaman seemed willing enough to give Eliana over to the chief a moment ago, he now held her back with a firm grip.

The dark figure said nothing else. His command had been given, and he stood there waiting. Eliana examined his back. He was clothed in some kind of synthetic cloth from head to foot, and a reflective helmet covered his head.

She didn't get to look long. The chief clenched his fists and lunged forward, dodging around the dark figure and closing the gap to Eliana in a couple strides. A vein bulged in his forehead as he advanced.

She instinctively brought her hands up in a feeble attempt to protect herself. Thinking he would barrel right through her, she tensed. But Amon's ring pulsed, and a wave of energy swept out of her hand, pulling at the air and whipping her hair into her eyes.

Everyone except Eliana and the dark man were thrown to the ground.

When her vision cleared, the chief was sprawled on his back, his decorative clothing torn and scattered in pieces beneath him. A bright, bloody scrape fanned out like road rash across his chest.

The dark figure morphed into a jaguar and shambled over toward the chief with a yawn, baring bloody yellowed teeth. The jungle cat and the chief locked eyes for a long moment. Then the chief inclined his head. The jaguar licked its lips and sauntered away, sitting patiently to one side.

Eliana felt her whole body go slack with fear. She sank to the ground and pushed dirt around with frantic feet until she felt a solid stone wall at her back. She pressed her hands to the cold stone. *Please,* she prayed, *let this be just another hallucination!*

The shaman stood and approached the chief. He asked him a question and held out his hand. The chief nodded and allowed the shaman to pull him to his feet.

They stood facing each other, the jaguar watching. The way the chief's shoulders slumped, Eliana thought he might be seeking an apology from his elder, who had shamed him before the others. The shaman seemed to accept the chief's apology, gripping his shoulders with gnarled hands and embracing him.

But then the shaman's eyes bulged, the color drained from his face, and when the chief stepped away he held a bloody shard of sharpened obsidian in his hand—the knife from the shaman's belt.

The jaguar growled and stepped toward the chief. The chief stared the cat down, an evil smirk twisting his mouth. Finally, the jaguar yowled into the night, then bounded into the jungle and disappeared.

Before she knew what was happening, the chief was barking orders at his men, and they were rushing around and past her. Two men returned with the remainder of the purple paint and the brushes they had used to paint Eliana. As they coated the gasping shaman's body with dye, they stripped him of his headdress and accoutrements with obvious haste.

The chief donned the headdress. He glanced at her for a moment, stepped forward. Then, seeming to change his mind, returned to his grim task.

Eliana curled her knees to her chest and pulled her legs tight. She wanted to run, but where would she go? Certainly not back to the dark cell. She fingered the diamond set into her ring. It was warm.

A moment later, the chief and his men were leading the shaman, brushed with purple paint and bleeding from the hole in his lower back, down the paved white path.

The chief's son separated from the group. He came over to Eliana and placed a damp rag in her hands.

She hurried after the villagers, afraid to be left alone in this strange jungle. She scrubbed at her skin as she followed, desperate to remove every trace of the purple paint.

The deep thrum of steady drums sounded and grew louder, reverberating and echoing off the stone walls and steps of the structures she passed. She could not help noticing that every wall, every stone staircase railing, was carved with elaborate reliefs and colored with chipped paint. Old, but not so old as to be forgotten.

The cracked path of white stones opened into a vast courtyard. She trembled, for a massive stepped pyramid rose into the night sky on the other side.

A thousand people or more gathered around the base of the pyramid, caught up in a riotous celebration. They danced and sang and mingled together to the beat of the drums.

Despite the humid air, Eliana gripped herself while she hurried around the edge of the courtyard. The loincloth she wore did little to suppress the shivers of fear that wracked her body.

Ixchel spotted her and rushed over. She took the wet cloth from Eliana's hand and scrubbed a few spots on her face until she was satisfied. Then she demanded a sarong from one of the other women who had clothing to spare and wrapped it around Eliana tightly, covering up the remainder of the purple paint as best she could. Most of the women, especially the younger ones, were sparely dressed. They stared at her and pointed without embarrassment for a moment then returned their attention to the ceremony.

The men had reached the base of the pyramid. Six figures climbed the steps. When they reached the summit, the chief—it must have been, for the shaman's headdress he wore was clearly outlined against the large moon—raised his arms. The obsidian knife in his hands glinted in the moonlight.

Four others bent the shaman backward over a block of stone, one man gripping each of his limbs. The chief called down a few words, a sonorous phrase directed at the crowd of people. Their feverish dancing slowed, gradually came to a stop. A hush washed over the courtyard.

Slowly, people raised hands into the air. Their thumbs and forefingers closed in circles, each of their other three fingers extended.

A-okay, Eliana thought.

The chief plunged his knife down then reached in and pulled out the former shaman's heart. As he smeared blood on a statue at the back of the platform the crowd erupted once again, and Eliana puked onto her purple feet.

8
LOCKDOWN

"THIS IS CRAZY," Reuben said. "You know that, right?"

They had parked Reuben's Ford Taurus in the middle of the parking lot in front of a monolithic white building with small windows. A round blue *NASA* logo occupied the highest corner of the front-facing wall.

"It's the only thing that makes sense," Amon said. He rubbed his thumb against the smooth plastic of the transponder prototype in one hand and sipped at the bitter gas station coffee they'd picked up on their way out of town with the other. He'd only slept two, maybe three hours out of the last forty-eight, but the caffeine and the short nap he took while Reuben drove into the hill country had given him a second wave of energy.

"Tell me again," Reuben said. "Why not call them like a normal person? Get one of NASA's nerds to send a sample down to our lab."

"It would take weeks to process a formal request. This is NASA we're talking about. Besides, if I had someone else send the sample, how could I be sure it was from the same meteorite?"

Reuben pursed his lips. "Valid point."

Amon stared out the window through a gap in the rows of cars parked in the lot, eyeballing the front door. Located about an hour outside of Austin, the building was three stories tall with zero character, belying the high-tech equipment kept inside. Keycard swipes marked three exits on the sides and back, and one in front.

NASA owned the building, but since the LTA was originally established as a division within NASA, the sister agencies often shared office space. Thus, Amon, through the Auriga Project, had been granted general access to this and several other NASA/LTA buildings.

"All I know is that Eliana was wearing that ring when she translocated," Amon said. "And I got the carbonado here. NASA retrieved the meteorite from Antarctica last year."

"A carbonado is nothing more than a funny-colored diamond. Why would a diamond throw the translocation off like that?"

"What difference does it make if it helps us find her?"

Reuben exhaled and nodded. "You're right, but..."

Amon leaned forward in his seat. "Were there always cameras on this building?"

"I don't know."

"I don't think there were. Wait a minute, that's Audrey, get down."

Amon first met Audrey when he interviewed her for a job at Fisk Industries over two years ago. They had discovered, to their mutual delight, that they were both fascinated with meteorites. She took the job at NASA, however, because Fisk Industries didn't focus on the kind of work she was passionate about. Amon had always respected that. They kept in touch and when the rare meteorite sample arrived in her lab, she sent Amon an excited email, inviting him down to check out her latest project.

Fortunately, Audrey didn't recognize Reuben's car or happen to glance down at the two men slouching in the front seats as she passed by their window.

As she approached the front door of the building, a man in a baseball cap and a black polo shirt opened the door from the inside.

"Since when did they get extra security guards?" Amon said.

"You're asking me?" Reuben said. "This is the first time I've ever been here."

"My keycard should still work. I'm going to try one of the side doors." Amon pulled the car door handle.

"Wait!" Reuben said. "Give me that thing." He held his hand out.

Amon looked down. He forgot he had been gripping the transponder. He handed it back and slipped out of the car.

He tried to appear casual as he stepped quickly between rows of cars, moving through the parking lot to the side of the building. A van door slid open and closed somewhere behind him. He maintained an even pace and kept his eyes down.

He rounded a corner of the building. At an unguarded side door, he pulled his wallet out of his pocket and pressed it against the black square reader. All Fisk Industries buildings had similar keycards securing their doors. They shared a common database of users, a list of every employee with access to a Fisk building. The card Amon kept in his wallet gave him access to all of them, but not necessarily to each room inside. He didn't, for instance, have access to the lab where the meteorites were stored, but he figured he'd cross that bridge when he came to it.

The signal light on top of the reader flashed red. Amon removed the card from the wallet and rubbed it against the reader without the leather of the wallet interfering. Again, a red signal light blinked.

"Dammit," he said.

"Mr. Fisk?" a voice called. A camera shutter snapped carelessly between wheezy breaths.

He smacked the card against the reader again, and again it was rejected.

"Dude, it *is* you," the voice said. Amon turned and gazed up at a large balding man. Camera straps dragged a windbreaker off his round shoulders. "I told my producer you wouldn't be all the way out here right now, not with what happened to your wife and all, but I've been camping out here anyhow. Shit, am I glad to be wrong. My name's Carter. Can I get a quote from you?"

Amon hurried around to another side of the building, trying not to make eye contact with the reporter. He snapped his card against the reader marking the back exit. Red denial winked back at him.

"Come on," Amon said.

The reporter caught up with him, wheezing harder. "Man, you're quick, dude. The footage of the accident is all over the Internet. I've watched it, like, a hundred times." Three more quick snaps of the camera shutter followed. "I can't imagine what you're going through right now." *Ch-chic ch-chic.*

Amon hurried back the way he'd come, skirting around the reporter and shielding his face. When he reached the corner, he broke into a sprint, finally slamming himself into the passenger seat of the Taurus and heaving the door shut behind him. Lynyrd Skynyrd crooned "Sweet Home Alabama" on the radio—Reuben liked the classics.

"I can't get in," he panted.

"What the hell is wrong with the front door?"

"Forget it. Let's go."

The reporter lumbered toward the car, two cameras swinging at his sides, his mouth wide and gasping for air like a guppy out of water.

The front door to the building swung open, and a security guard peered out to check on the commotion. He watched the reporter run like Chris Farley in a sketch comedy then took out a cell phone and held it to his ear.

"But you told me—" Reuben objected.

The reporter slid into the side of the Taurus. He held a business card to the window and asked Amon a question made unintelligible by his panting. *Statesman*, the card read, the name of an Austin-based newspaper.

"Go!" Amon yelled.

Reuben ratcheted the column shifter into gear and sped off.

Amon wiped his sweaty palms on his jeans the whole way back to the city. "Something's going on here, Reuben, something bad."

"You probably just demagnetized your card with your cell phone. Happens to me all the time."

"No, I always keep them separate."

"Okay. Well, someone could have revoked your priority on accident, maybe?"

"What about that reporter camping out there? He said he didn't think I was going to be there, but someone must have tipped him off."

Reuben pressed his tongue against the inside of his cheek. "Did he say who?"

"I didn't stop long enough to ask."

"Look, we'll get the keycard fixed and come back tomorrow. No harm, no foul."

"Something about it doesn't feel right."

Reuben flexed his fingers on the steering wheel. "What are you thinking?" he asked.

"I don't know. Maybe you're right, and I'm being paranoid," Amon said. "Can I change the station?"

Reuben nodded, keeping his eyes on the road.

Amon flipped the radio from classic rock to an AM band news channel.

The voice of Reagan Gruber, the controversial ultraconservative radio personality, floated through the speakers. "Are you really surprised? His own wife vanishes into thin air *on camera* and you expect the program to continue to be funded? ON CAMERA. Of course the Lunar Terraform Alliance doesn't want anything to do with him now. Of course they should shut him down—and confiscate that unstable, irresponsible contraption. This is a matter of public safety, and the *Hopper*, as that nut job affectionately calls his invention, is a danger to us all."

They could tell from blocks away that a furor of activity had taken hold of the campus. It was unusually busy for a weekday afternoon: media vans parked haphazardly in the fire lane in front of the headquarters building with spotlights and cameras prepared and electrical equipment jacked in to solar cells Fisk Industries had probably manufactured. Two pairs of police patrol cars kept tabs on the growing crowd from a reasonable distance.

"Good thing we're in *my* car," Reuben said. "I'll park on the east end of the campus. We can get into the labs through Solar R&D without anyone noticing."

That turned out to be wishful thinking. Lookouts had been stationed at every entrance, and by the time they reached the entrance to Solar R&D, a mob of hungry-eyed, microphone-waving reporters bore down upon them.

Amon slammed his wallet into the card reader. The light flashed green, and the door opened inward. Reuben hurried in behind him, and they heaved the doors shut. Two reporters squeezed through, barking after them, but they managed to extricate themselves with the help of a couple Fisk Industries employees who spotted Amon and Reuben and ran to their aid.

"See," Amon said to Reuben under his breath once they were out of earshot, "I told you my card wasn't demagnetized."

Reuben harrumphed.

At the entrance to the underground physics labs, an entirely different kind of chaos held sway. Lucas stood at the head of a gathering of scientists with Wes at his shoulder. He was telling them that their careers at Fisk Industries had come to an abrupt and irrevocable end.

"Without funding from the Lunar Terraform Alliance," said Lucas, straining to be heard over the hubbub of objections and curses, "we can't keep you all on."

"I've dedicated years to Fisk Industries!" someone yelled from the back.

"We know," said Wes. "And you'll be generously compensated for your service."

"This is bullshit!" said Jeanine, which made Amon smile. "Ten years of hard work laid to waste by one single screw-up. And we weren't *really* even given a chance to figure out—"

When she saw Amon, she stopped midsentence. Her mouth fell open, her cheeks turned red. "Amon, I'm so sorry," she said.

"Why?" he said, giving Wes and Lucas a glare. "Everything you said is true. This *is* bullshit. We *weren't* given a chance to figure out what went wrong with the Translocator. That's why no one is being let go."

"Amon," Wes said, staring him down. "This isn't your decision."

"It certainly isn't yours."

"What do you know!?" said Wes, jabbing Amon in the chest. "Have you brought four companies back from the brink of bankruptcy? Have you spent the last two weeks patching the holes in this sinking ship? While you were tinkering with equations in your lab, Lucas and I were busy keeping *your* company afloat."

Amon held his shaking hands behind his back. Bad luck didn't come in threes. It used the first three hellish stabs to get you on the ground then kicked your teeth in while you bled out in the dirt.

"*I* know what needs to be done to salvage this company," Wes continued. "Fisk Industries wouldn't exist if it wasn't for *my* capital and *my* political connections."

"No one funded us for how well we can give a speech, Wes. They funded us for our research and our solar panels."

Lucas pressed his hands together in front of his chest, beseeching Amon to listen. "Please, Amon, we can't afford to pay these scientists without funding from the LTA."

"The LTA will change their tune when we identify the problem with the Translocator and fix it." *And find Eliana*. His eyes seesawed between Lucas' downcast face and the twinkle of avarice in Wes's eyes. Of course they had been working together—Wes was a master at manipulating good-hearted people like Lucas. It made him immensely sad that those who were supposed to help protect the company were so eager to dismantle it.

"No, they won't," said Wes.

A chill ran down Amon's spine. Wes seemed too sure. He turned on Lucas. "Did you tell him?"

"N—no," Lucas said. "I swear."

"Tell me what?" Wes demanded.

"Are you working with them?" Amon shot back.

"With who?"

"With whoever is behind this trap!"

Wes McManis cocked his head like a computing machine, calculating with precision, searching for weakness. "You're losing it, aren't you? Paranoia. Anger. When was the last time you slept? You need to get some rest."

"I *need* to find Eliana. And you need to back the fuck off." The words tumbled out before he caught them. Amon felt his eyes bulge.

Wes edged back. "You really are losing it."

Amon swung his head around, looking for support, but even Jeanine was looking at him warily out of the corners of her eyes, like he was a rabid dog.

Over Wes's shoulder, Amon saw Fowler and Montoya step around the corner. Half a dozen more men and women trailed them, wearing plastic gloves and carrying forensic kits and computer bags. A cargo mule drone brought up the rear of the procession.

Amon took note of the equipment. Despite his misgivings about Fowler and Montoya, this was certainly the FBI's *modus operandi*. They couldn't take the arch with that crew, but they could lug away critical equipment, disabling the Hopper until they returned with a large enough container to commandeer the rest. Judging by the size and kind of containers they chose—for, certainly, the drone's cargo storage had a built-in Faraday cage and a thick layer of electrical insulation—they knew exactly what they were looking for. They'd pack up the main control unit, download the translocation data, and wipe the local backups.

It would be as if his research had never existed.

He kept redundant backups for emergencies, but Amon wouldn't be able to recover from the hardware sabotage. He couldn't let that happen.

Amon grabbed Wes by the shirt and pulled him close. Spit flew into Wes's face as he snarled, and he didn't care how crazy it made him look. "You bastard," he said. "You knew they were coming."

Wes only smiled. Amon shoved him back and glared at Lucas. He couldn't be mad at his old friend like he could at Wes. With Lucas, he was simply disappointed that he had let himself be taken advantage of.

Finally, Amon took Reuben aside and whispered in his ear, "Watch your email."

With no further warning, Amon juked through the gathering of startled scientists and sprinted toward the lab.

Montoya saw him move first. "Hey!" he shouted.

The crowd of loyal scientists and researchers closed ranks behind him, blocking Montoya and giving Amon a head start. Amon pumped his arms down the corridor, pausing long enough to throw any fire doors he passed shut behind him.

The fire doors would merely slow them down. There was only one door that would keep them out. One door, for security purposes, that wasn't hardwired to the main grid.

He skidded to a halt inside the automatic glass doors leading to Hopper's lab. The automatic doors sighed closed behind him. At the control unit, Amon keyed in the lockdown code only he knew. Electromagnets released the blast door, a three-foot-thick wall of solid steel. It dropped into place over the lab's normal glass door one inch at a time, agonizingly slow.

Overhead, charges went off in a series of pops and hisses, welding the rooftop telescope opening, which had been used for the demonstration, permanently shut.

Montoya made it to the end of the long hall. The automatic doors to the lab had been locked when the blast door was released, so they didn't slide open as Montoya approached. He punched the glass and paced back, made as if to draw something from his jacket, then seemed to change his mind as someone called his attention from behind.

Through his only shrinking window to the outside world, Amon waved to Montoya. Fowler came up behind him. She stared at Amon with barely contained rage.

The blast door finally reached the floor and sealed into place with a heavy thunk.

9
LIFE IN KAKUL

WHEN THE CHIEF and his men descended from the pyramid after the midnight sacrifice had been performed, the crowd of painted, drunk natives held aloft the lifeless body of the shaman and followed a different paved road into the jungle. Eliana refused to follow them, so Ixchel waited patiently with her. When the villagers returned a short time later, they came back empty handed.

Then the villagers exited on the opposite side of the ruined city. Eliana went with them this time, gathering her wits, the taste of vomit fresh in her mouth. She walked down a narrow dirt trail through the jungle to a village built a couple hundred yards back from the cliff's sheer edge.

An entire village of thatched, adobe-walled huts housing nearly a thousand people, and Eliana had deduced no sign of its existence when she first arrived. She shook her head when she saw it, incredulous that she had once imagined this place uninhabited.

In the weeks following the midnight sacrifice, Eliana established a precarious place for herself among the indigenous population. Whether this was allowed by Chief

Dambu—for, eventually, she learned that was the name of the chief who had tried to attack her—or she was overlooked because Ixchel and the chief's youngest son fell ill, she could never be sure.

She kept a wary guard for the first couple days, startling awake at the sound of the wind. No one tried to imprison her again or even cause her any harm. Instead, they let her be, following the chief's example and giving her a wide berth like she was some kind of leper or witch.

They must have thought she was, for children froze and stared when they crossed her path until their mothers ran back to haul them away. And when she went to the river for water, people watched her fearfully, their eyes darting to her hand where Amon's ring was visible.

Her best guess was that word got around about what happened with the ring, how it protected her from the chief and caused everyone else to be thrown to the ground. She didn't for a minute think this special protection would last, but her survival depended on her fitting in, and she wasted no time wondering. These people were her only source of food and shelter, not to mention knowledge of how to survive in this world. The longer they ignored her, the worse off she would be.

The first thing to do—a smart survival tactic in any new community—was to stake a claim. Something that could establish her place without infringing on The Way Things Are, or threaten the safety of the community.

Eliana chose an abandoned hut at the outskirts of the village. She swept the dirt floor and made a bed for herself out of grass and a ratty old blanket. It was shabby compared to the fired adobe mounds on which the nicer family complexes were constructed, like the one occupied by

Ixchel and Dambu near the center of the village. Eliana's thatched roof leaked, and she had to build a dam out of big logs to direct the water out the door when it rained, which it seemed to do every night. At least it was something she could call her own.

Away from the stone city, the natives washed the paint from their faces and dressed more plainly. Religious ceremonies took a backseat to a life of farming and crafting. Men spent their days tending the fields adjacent to their family home or hunting wild turkeys in the jungle, while women weaved and cooked and made pottery and cared for the children. The entire village also took turns tending large shared crops of—unmistakably—corn.

When the boy fell ill, Ixchel's household did not participate in the shared work. Eliana dared not go near the house, for *incensarios* burning tree resin constantly spilled thick white smoke into the air, and Ixchel and Dambu both lingered around the house mournfully, neither working nor cleaning. Others tended their gardens and brought them any supplies they needed—food, water, clean clothes—while they prayed for the gods to heal their youngest son, Tilak.

On the second night after the ceremony, Eliana saw Chief Dambu decapitate a small bird and spread its blood along the door frame—a ward against evil or a prayer, or maybe a little of both.

The next morning, Eliana resolved to find a way to get closer to people, to make friends, to learn their language so she could make sense of their customs.

The first thing to do, then, was hide her ring out of sight so it didn't draw stares. She adopted the native style of dress after the younger women, tying one loincloth around her waist and another under her arms.

After giving it some consideration, her best option was to find a piece of string to hold the ring around her neck, long enough to conceal it beneath the half shirt, and later beneath a dress if she acquired one. So she climbed up on a log and searched the thatched roof of her hut for a piece of string that would be suitable. She found one and stretched out to reach it when a voice startled her.

She lost her balance on the log and fell.

A young man caught her. She hadn't seen him close up since the night of the ceremony—as Ixchel's oldest son, he, too, had been involved in the prayer for and care of the sick Tilak.

He glanced at the ring on her hand, but he didn't freeze like the children or beat a hasty retreat like the other adults. He smiled at her now, looking like nothing more than the awkward teenager he was.

"Uh, hi," she said.

After a moment's hesitation where she regained her feet, Eliana recalled the words that Ixchel taught her. "*Bix a k'aaba*?" she said.

"Rakulo," he said. Then pointed at her. "Eliana?"

She nodded.

Rakulo helped her reach the string she'd found. He seemed to relax a little when the ring was out of sight beneath her tunic, proving her theory to be correct. He even helped her repair the part of her roof that leaked. She supposed that was what brought him over in the first place—he thought she was trying to fix the roof. She didn't complain. The leak was bad, and she had no idea how to fix it on her own.

They communicated in gestures well enough. Body language went a long way. But when she asked for him to show her around, gesturing toward the village and putting her arm through his, he backed away, shaking his head, and left.

She interpreted this to mean that she was still not welcome in the village. Eliana spent the rest of that afternoon walking back down the beach to where she had first arrived. She took the path she had seen men take when they left in the early mornings carrying fishing lines in their hands. It switchbacked down a sloping hill to the rocky end of the beach.

Amon's name was long gone when she reached the spot where she had first arrived. She would have walked right past it if it weren't for the sticks she'd left marking its place, one of which had been knocked over. Eliana straightened the sticks, pressing them deep into the sand, and carved his name again with a sharp rock she carried from the cliff.

Willing him to come for her didn't make him appear, however, and when the sun began to set she made her way back so she didn't have to climb the narrow trail up to the village in the dark.

The moons shone through the violet twilight several handspans apart. The larger satellite was about three-quarters full. It seemed to have waned much faster than the smaller moon, whose full face had only lost a pale-red sliver.

The next morning, Rakulo came back to Eliana's hut accompanied by a teenage girl named Citlali. Eliana bemoaned the fact that she was stuck at the phase of language acquisition where all she could learn were names, but her luck changed that morning.

As Citlali led Eliana into the village, she realized that Rakulo's discomfort at the idea of showing her around wasn't personal. It was simply that it was improper in their culture for an unmarried young man to be seen with a woman alone—though she was married on Earth, they had no way to know that. During her tour with Citlali, Eliana learned that the single young men in the tribe stayed together in a large house, like a bunkhouse on a ranch. Presumably, they stayed there until they married and started a family of their own. The single young women, however, stayed with their parents.

It was to Citlali's parents' home that they went, and to her delight Eliana was immediately put to work with almost no explanation. Citlali was young enough to be Eliana's daughter, but her experience with the daily chores made Eliana seem practically incompetent by comparison.

Citlali instructed her with gestures and one-word phrases. "*Ha*," she said as she shoved a heavy clay pot into Eliana's arms and pointed her toward the river. *Ha* meant water. Eliana gladly fetched it, and upon her return she was sent back twice more. After the third pot, she held her lower back with her hand and groaned, and Citlali glanced sideways at her with disdain.

Eliana learned the word for no was *ma* when she nearly emptied out a shallow bowl of corn husks, thinking it was meant to be disposed of. Citlali gestured angrily, speaking rapidly, her speech full of glottal stops, harsh fricatives, and elongated vowels.

Citlali's mother smiled and gently took the bowl from Eliana, returning it to its place on the porch. Nothing went to waste here.

Larger families like Citlali's lived and worked together in a complex—for lack of a better word—consisting of two, three, or sometimes four thatch-roofed huts per family. The largest building served as the domicile, where they slept and ate. The clay mounds on which the houses were built were larger than the houses, and the roofs extended out as well, giving the residents a shaded porch to stay cool while they worked. Nearby, another building served as a kitchen and dining room, and a third, usually open to the air, served as a workshop—whether it was used to shape pots of clay or pull fibers from a plant that looked like some kind of cactus, but which Eliana eventually identified as agave. Small plots of yams, beans, and other colorful vegetables were planted adjacent to the house in any area that wasn't being used for something else. Eliana was perplexed when she noticed that some fields went unused and untouched but learned that the fields were being rotated.

It was as if an entire village in ancient Central America had been lifted from the pages of history and set down on this planet wholly intact.

She quickly grew used to living among them. Citlali's family fed her and clothed her in exchange for her labor, and Eliana did her best to show her thanks any way she could.

Why the village was out here, on the edge of the cliff, instead of in the stone city where the sacrifice ceremony took place continued to nag at her mind. As an archaeologist, she knew that many suspected that people lived in those stone cities when they were built in the Americas. So why did these people not seem to want anything to do with the place unless a specific ceremony was at hand? Did the city have a different meaning here? Why live in thatch-roofed huts when palaces of stone, which could house the entire village with room to spare, existed not a mile away?

She found no answer to these questions in her days with Citlali, and yet she couldn't bring herself to explore far on her own. The very thought of the stone city sent chills running up her spine. The fact that she saw Chief Dambu walking into the jungle many times, carrying armfuls of household goods and the occasional small bird, did nothing to assuage her fears. She dreaded facing him alone again. She had no faith that the ring would save her a second time.

Citlali's family home was situated close to Dambu and Ixchel. It was, in fact, Citlali's family primarily who fed them while Tilak lay ill.

One day, about a month after she met Citlali (she still used Earth units to keep track of the passage of time), Citlali's mother instructed her to take a container of tamales wrapped in corn husks to Ixchel. Eliana was honored by the assignment. Usually, Citlali or one of the other girls would deliver the food.

However, Eliana never got the chance to speak with Ixchel. When she came within sight of the chief's home, Rakulo and Dambu burst from the main hut of their family complex. Rakulo shoved Dambu in the chest. Dambu pulled his son's face close and screamed at Rakulo, spit flying, his voice thick with emotion. Eliana had picked up a smattering of the language by now, but they spoke so rapidly she couldn't understand them at all. Rakulo was ill prepared for a battle of raw strength, and his father quickly overcame him. Dambu swung big meaty fists, bloodying Rakulo's nose and sending him sprawling to the ground.

Ixchel emerged from the hut behind them. She held a small, limp body in her arms, and tears streamed down her face.

It was Ixchel's youngest son, Tilak, the same boy that had surprised Eliana on the beach the very first day. Ixchel fell to her knees in the yard. She laid the boy down and straightened his arms and legs. He didn't breath. His eyes stared up, unmoving. The men stopped fighting and kneeled at the boy's side.

Ixchel closed her son's eyelids for the last time.

Then a cry filled with grief like Eliana had never heard rose up from Ixchel's throat and erupted into the soft noise of the village like the siren of the damned, a great wail, like her soul was being torn from her body.

She threw herself on the ground and shed hot tears on the cold body of her son.

Rakulo tried to comfort her. She pushed him away.

Dambu, his face a mask, did not even try to console his wife. He didn't look capable of it. He stood and turned and stalked off into the jungle once more.

10
THREATS AND INTIMIDATION

AMON PACED INTO the lounge for the umpteenth time. Years ago, while studying for his master's at Stanford, he'd acquired the nervous habit of visiting the fridge. It helped to distract him and clear his mind before plunging back into a difficult or sticky problem. The habit was noticeably less helpful, and a bit more painful, however, when he was dealing with a limited supply of food, and none of it fresh.

He had lucked out the day he locked himself inside the lab. The kitchenette adjacent to the lounge had been recently stocked by the caterers, who came every two weeks. They left enough coffee, snacks, energy drinks, and protein bars to feed a team of fifteen people. Factored in with the various meals the staff had left behind, Amon calculated that he could stretch the supplies out for eight weeks. He'd been in the lab for forty-five days, so he was well into week six now.

He ran his fingers along his chin, pulling at coarse, uneven stubble. "When I get out of here I'm never eating another protein bar again," he said to no one in particular. The habit of talking to himself...well, that one he'd acquired more recently.

Eliana had been missing for sixty-one days. Each moment without her felt like a failure, but he forced himself to keep track. He didn't want to know how much he was letting her down, but he wasn't in the habit of letting his own dishonesty blind him to the truth either.

For something different, he emptied half a package of dried ramen noodles into a bowl, filled it with water from the sink, and stuck it in the microwave. This was a treat. He only had four ramen noodle packages left, and he was hoarding them.

Amon returned to the computer with the steaming bowl in one hand. He pulled up the console program and ran the hacked satellite relay script he used to communicate with Reuben. It was the first thing he'd set up when he locked himself inside the lab. The script was originally developed to communicate with the Lunar Station, but Amon had modified it to send messages to Reuben's personal email. He also added an extra layer of encryption. Not foolproof, but to crack it you had to know where to look. He typed in a long password, plus a two-step verification code sent to a separate machine over the WiFi. Reuben used a similar setup on his end.

The cursor jumped down to a new line, and he typed:

> *NEWS?*

Then pressed *Enter* and waited.

When Amon first got in touch through the encrypted messaging system, he told Reuben how to find Audrey, the scientist in the meteorite studies department at NASA whom he'd first examined the meteorite sample with, and who gave Amon the carbonado for Eliana's ring. They agreed that Reuben would tell Audrey a fake story about doing independent studies of his own and that he wanted to compare the carbonado samples to some in his personal collection. Certain departments at NASA and Fisk Industries shared interests, so this wouldn't by any means be flagged as an unusual request.

But when Audrey tried to bring Reuben into the facility, it triggered some flag in their new security system that caused his access to be inexplicably denied at the door, and he left empty handed.

Since then, Reuben had filed a formal request—a bureaucratic black box that promised to bury his efforts in endless reviews and appeals—and, more recently, resorted to stalking around outside the facility at night looking for ways to get in.

Amon was starting to worry about Reuben. But he didn't see another way.

Five minutes later, words appeared on his screen:

> *PURGATORY. STILL DOING RECON. LOOKING AT OTHER OPTIONS.*

Amon sighed. Purgatory meant the formal request still hovered in a gray void of bureaucracy, faceless and lost. The other part of the message must mean that Reuben was continuing his stakeout of the NASA facility in between maintaining appearances as a regular Fisk Industries employee. Instead of letting Reuben go, they'd transferred him to Solar R&D. A lot to juggle for any one man.

> *HOW ARE YOU HOLDING UP?*

> *CALLED IN SICK TODAY.*

> *WON'T THEY GET SUSPICIOUS?*

> *DO YOU HAVE A BETTER IDEA?*

Amon drew a blank. He'd forgiven Lucas and Wes for not telling him the FBI agents had arrived the day he locked himself in the lab. After he had time to think about it, he came to the conclusion that they'd done the right thing cooperating, even if Wes had been a damned sneak about it. Their leadership had to be defined by clear guidelines, remaining always within legal boundaries and doing what they perceived to be in the best interests of the company.

What Amon chose to do was his own choice. He'd come to terms with that. But that didn't leave him anyone else to turn to in this regard. He typed back to Reuben, feeling like a corrupt program stuck on a loop.

> *NO. BE CAREFUL.*

Amon signed off. One keystroke cleared the message history; another shut the program down.

Amon got up from the computer and went across the room to the far wall where a star map centered on the range of Eliana's possible locations. Blown up that large, the star map image was grainy, as if it had been expanded beyond its original dimensions. In reality, the galaxy he suspected she jumped to was thousands of light-years wide and billions of miles away. Good photos were not in abundance.

It took an hour after he'd locked himself in the lab to figure out that his team was no closer to pinpointing Eliana's exact location than they had been the last time he'd checked in. Since then, he compiled a list of over thirty-five exoplanets in what astronomers called "Goldilocks zones"—the range from the sun that supported life—of their respective solar systems where Eliana could have ended up. This odious work went slower on his own, and he missed his team of brilliant scientists.

The planets on his list weren't necessarily habitable planets. They were a good bet, but nothing was certain. And to make matters worse, for every planet NASA's satellites had identified as Earth-like, there were a thousand it hadn't yet discovered.

Amon rubbed his eyes in frustration. Even with a narrowed list of planets, it was impossible to tell which was the right one. His best guess was based on his team's statistical analysis. Their translocation calculations simply fell apart when applied across distances this vast. Eliana could have reassembled on any one of those planets in that section of space.

Or not.

That was assuming the machine could handle a translocation across that distance. It couldn't. Not without the meteorite sample, which Amon still suspected—and couldn't yet prove—had affected her translocation.

He slammed his fist down on the desk and cursed when he hit a days-old bruise. Not for the first time, he considered alternative ways to obtain a meteorite sample. If Reuben couldn't get his hands on one, he would have to find another way.

He walked across the lab to where the second mobile transponder prototype lay in pieces on its own table. On this, he'd made better progress.

The transponder still wasn't fully operational. Even if it was, a translocation required two people. If Amon reassembled outside of the lab with the transponder in hand—say, in the NASA facility where the meteorites were kept—someone would have to activate the Hopper from this side to bring him back.

Reuben could do it. But that would require getting him into the lab, which required a working transponder. Reuben insisted he could fix up the older prototype Amon left in his car, based on detailed instructions Amon had already sent, but that was only a couple days ago, and he'd been so focused on the meteorite sample he hadn't done so yet. In the meantime—

The internal teleconference line rang. Amon hurried over to the computer.

"What?" he said irritably after answering with voice only.

"I'm afraid I have some bad news, Amon," Lucas said.

"Of course you do. Are Fowler and Montoya still out there?"

"Montoya arrived for his shift a moment ago."

"Tell him to suck a bag of dicks. How does the FBI like paying overtime for a grown man to babysit me?"

"I heard that," Montoya said. "But you're stuck in that metal box, drinking your own piss, so the joke's on you."

Lucas interrupted them before Amon could fire back a sarcastic retort. "That isn't productive," he said. "I just came from the board meeting. It's official. They voted to remove you as CEO on the fiduciary responsibility clause, as we expected. They appointed me acting CEO, and Wes McManis agreed to take a bigger role in the day-to-day activities of the company."

"Did he agree, or did he worm his way in there?"

"Either way, we need the help."

Amon made a noncommittal sound in the back of his throat. "What about the cutbacks?"

"Solar manufacturing is at 60 percent capacity. We had to let a few more people go. We gave the order to temporarily close the manufacturing facilities in Beijing."

"Shit."

"The deals with Intel and GE got called off. Other divisions are operating at half manpower. Repair calls are running an endless backlog."

"You couldn't save Beijing?"

"We had no choice, Amon. Cash flow is tight. If we don't make these cuts now, in a few months it will be a worse situation. And with our overhead..."

"What about a line of credit?"

"You think anyone would give us a loan after all the bad press we've had?"

Amon sighed. "I wish there was more I could do."

"You could come out of there," Lucas said.

"Not going to happen."

"The bad press would calm down once this whole lockdown situation is no longer a spectacle. We'd be able to start a marketing campaign to reinvent our image, pick support of our products back up, revisit some of the industrial deals that got shut down after the... accident."

"And what about Eliana?"

A moment of silence passed between them.

"Fine," Lucas said. "Don't take my advice."

"Have you heard from Dr. Badeux? You said he was going to call me. I haven't heard anything."

"That's what he told me, but I haven't heard from him either. I'll reach out to him again. The LTA's PR team has been trying desperately to disassociate themselves from the accident."

"Yet they collude with the FBI to ruin me."

"They put a lot into this project, Amon. They're just doing what they think needs to be done to protect their reputation."

Amon choked back an angry retort. He understood that logic, but something about it still didn't sit right.

Lucas said he had to get across town for a meeting, so Amon disconnected the call and checked again for a message from Reuben. There wasn't one.

The teleconference line rang again. This time, it was Fowler.

"You can't last forever in there, Amon," she reminded him.

"How many times are you going to tell me that?"

"As many as it takes. My offer of a deal still stands."

"How do I know you won't try to dismantle the Translocator like you did before?"

"You can keep searching for your wife for the next three months. That was the deal. After that, whether your find her or not, you turn over the Translocator to me."

Amon scoffed. "Thanks, but no thanks. Oh, and tell your lapdog he can go home any time. I'm not budging."

He disconnected that call as well and paced back into the lounge. Despite his growling stomach, he forced himself to return to his workstation empty handed. The longer he could make his supplies last, the better odds Reuben had to do what needed to be done.

The digital clock on his computer read *7:05* when he got his next message from Reuben.

> *I'M SORRY.*

Amon typed back with shaking fingers.

> *WHAT HAPPENED? WHY?*

> *REUBEN????*

When he didn't respond, Amon pulled up a VoIP line on the computer. It was less secure than his chat program, but he took the chance and dialed the number for Reuben's burner phone. They had avoided talking on the phone because it was likely to be recorded. Fisk Industries policy was against recording calls, but that didn't mean it wasn't possible for someone else to do so.

"Hello?" Reuben answered, fear pulling his voice taught.

"Reuben, it's me."

"They're onto me, kid."

"What the hell happened?"

"It's not safe anymore."

"What do you mean? What happened?"

"A man broke into my house. Attacked me. He said he'd—" Reuben's voice cracked as he choked out the word, "kill Charlie in his sleep and make it look like an accident if I didn't stop snooping around."

"He's bluffing, Reuben."

"How can you be so sure? They came to where I live. They threatened Charlie. I never told anyone where he was staying. Not even you. But they know."

Amon felt a fist of guilt wrap its leaden fingers around his aching heart. Here he was in the awkward position of asking his friend to help him rescue Eliana, when Reuben had been suffering the loss of his own partner in slow, jagged spoonfuls of anguish for the past year. The Alzheimer's had come swiftly and hit him hard. Instead of feeling angry that his friend was now abandoning him, Amon felt nothing but empathy. If anyone knew what Amon was going through, it was Reuben.

Amon didn't know what the right thing to say was, so he said what he always told his employees when he was at a loss for words: "We'll think of something."

Reuben choked back a sob. "Charlie doesn't even know who I am most days. But he's got no one else."

The lead fingers gripping Amon's heart squeezed. "Eliana needs you, too," he said. "*I* need you."

"I can't help you anymore," Reuben said. "You have to understand."

Amon took a deep breath. "I do understand, Reuben. But listen. I've got it all figured out. We can get Eliana back and be done with this in a day or two."

"I can't. Not now."

"Yes, now! If we don't get that meteorite sample, she's a goner."

Silence from the other end.

"Reuben?" No response. "Reuben!"

"I'm sorry," said Reuben. "Please understand. I have to keep him safe."

The line went dead. Amon let his head fall onto the tabletop, not even trying to soften the blow.

Yes, he thought. *I understand very well.*

11
UCHBEN NA

THEY FILLED THE dead boy's mouth with ground maize and a jade bead and buried him in a small mound behind the family home. Into the grave they reverently placed wooden effigies, a ball, a fishing line. Over it they lit incense and said prayers. Dambu decapitated another bird.

Ixchel's heart-rending public displays of grief lasted for several weeks following the funeral. She painted black stripes on her body and limbs with an ink made from crushed insects and flowers. She fasted, drinking only water and tea for sustenance, and grew thin. Sobs bubbled from her domicile each evening long into the night. Shortly before sunrise, a prolonged wail carried across the village. When she emerged from her pole and thatch hut, she sobbed quietly, discreetly, over the boy's grave and on her aimless, shambling walks through the village.

Rakulo spent a lot of his time with her. His grief was distinctly less vocal, yet his presence seemed to do nothing to ease his mother's pain.

As for Dambu, Eliana only saw his back as he stalked off into the jungle. Citlali said that was Dambu's way of grieving. Eliana suspected that she, too, would give space to Ixchel in the throes of her grief.

Rakulo accompanied Dambu on long outings a few times. Once they were gone for three days. They always came back empty handed and with a grim look on their faces. They were not in the jungle hunting wild turkeys like other men who went in the same direction.

Eliana spent her days with Citlali. She was younger than Eliana by a decade, but wiser than her by a lifetime in terms of life in the village of *Kakul*. Eliana quizzed her relentlessly, absorbing knowledge like a cracked desert floor does water.

She learned the word for every plant and object she could find, repeating them to Citlali over and over and over again. She had no paper to write on, and the only way to get comfortable with a language—she knew from her years taking Spanish in high school and German in college—was to use it. She hoarded words and phrases.

Some were familiar. Most of the natives smoked *sic*, tobacco, and the act of smoking was *sicar*, close enough to cigar to be an obvious loanword to English. When rain fell, it was referred to as a *junrakan*, which sounded an awful lot like hurricane. Whether this word referred to the storm or the God of Storms who sent it, Eliana was never quite certain. The natives seemed to use the ideas interchangeably. So the word for hurricane could be used in both contexts: "A *junrakan* is coming" and "Praise *Junrakan*! I don't have to carry another pot of water all the way from the river to water the garden."

The jungle was *k'aax*, with the soft shushing sound at the end; the beach, *jaal*. They referred to the world with the word *kab*, but to the dirt or the earth as *lu'um*. The sky they called *ka'an*.

"And what do your people call themselves?" Eliana asked Citlali one day while they were washing laundry in a calm eddy of the river.

"*Kakuli*," she said, submerging a loincloth and scrubbing it clean beneath the water.

"Ah, I see. Like the village, *Kakul*?"

Citlali nodded.

Eliana's mouth went dry at the next question that came to her mind, but the need to know egged her onward.

"And what do you call the village of stones?" she asked, referring to the ruined city with the pyramid at its heart.

Citlali leaned close. "*Uchben Na*," she whispered. *Ancient Mother.*

Eliana shivered.

They returned to *Kakul* with the clean laundry in their arms, the waterlogged clothes a heavier burden on their return journey despite their best efforts to ring the cloth out.

Upon their return, Eliana was surprised to find Ixchel sitting in the midst of a group of women, grinding maize in a stone bowl and laughing at the children who played tag and kicked a ball around within sight of their mothers.

Eliana glanced at Citlali, who shrugged. Citlali was practical, laconic of speech, and unfazed by most things.

"Hello, girls," Ixchel said as they approached.

Citlali inclined her head respectfully and went on with her work while Eliana nearly dropped the heavy pot she carried.

"Hello," she stammered. The women chuckled.

The black stripes on Ixchel's arms remained, but they had begun to fade. She was noticeably thinner but otherwise seemed unmarked by her recent grief. Regaining the weight would be a matter of weeks, if not days, of a regular diet. If Ixchel was here, she was likely to have broken her fast already.

It was as if the abyss of sadness she fell into over the past several weeks unburdened her of the death of her son.

"Come," Ixchel said.

Eliana tiptoed over, scared of what might happen. Perhaps she had been wrong. Ixchel beckoned with open arms, setting the stone bowl aside.

When she approached, Ixchel seized Eliana's face in both hands, inspecting her like a doctor. She grunted then pinched the twine around Eliana's neck and pulled her ring from beneath her wrap. The women to either side of Ixchel tensed and shifted when the carbonado came into sight, but Ixchel didn't flinch.

"Mmm…it is beautiful," Ixchel said, holding it up to the sky, pulling a little on Eliana's neck. "Do not lose this, child. Xucha smiles upon you."

Eliana cocked her head. Why Xucha? These people seemed to have a god for every element. What was so special about that one? She dared not question Ixchel in front of all the other women.

And then it hit her: Xucha was a word the old shaman had spoken right before the jaguar stepped into the cell. The same jaguar who had faced Dambu down before Dambu put a knife in the shaman's back. Eliana had not seen another shaman in the village since then.

She didn't have time to consider it further, for Ixchel dropped the ring and began giving orders. Eliana hurriedly stuffed her makeshift necklace back into her shirt. Suddenly, there were a million things to do. Ixchel announced they were preparing for something big, that there were many days of work ahead of them.

Eliana still missed many words in rapid speech, so there were large gaps in her understanding, and she came to realizations slower than the others. After some time she figured out that it must be some kind of party or ceremony for which they were preparing.

Eliana panicked and rushed over to where Citlali nonchalantly de-feathered a turkey.

"What we are making..." Eliana said, considering her words carefully. "Is it for Ixchel, because she is well again?"

Citlali chuckled.

"For her son?"

"No," she said. "It is a party to celebrate the full moons."

Chills ran down Eliana's spine. "In... *Uchben Na*?"

Citlali shook her head once, firmly. "No. That comes later."

A shuddering breath escaped Eliana's lips. She sat down, blinking black dots from her vision. Citlali continued to pluck feathers from the bird. She offered no words of comfort.

Still, it was strange about Ixchel. They must really care for her. Eliana had taken the past several weeks to be indicative of the way the village operated. Perhaps she had been wrong. It seemed now as if the world had been on hold while Ixchel grieved her dead son.

And with her return, life began anew.

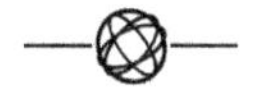

Ixchel and the other women kept Eliana at the ready and always moving for a solid week. A big feast was prepared, fruit-based alcoholic drinks were retrieved from stills stored in the forests. Eliana did anything they asked her to do. She ran errands, she cleaned, she picked up after them. They even let her do some of the cooking.

Ixchel took her on a journey collecting flowers, seeds, and leaves from particular locations scattered throughout *Kakul* and along the river. A hundred yards from the waterfall where the river spilled into the ocean, in shallow caves at the water's edge, they collected mushrooms.

Eliana's grasp on the language increased exponentially while she was forced to interact so closely and work with the other women from dawn till dusk. She achieved a new plateau of understanding. By the end of the week, with focus, patience, and heaping handfuls of corrections from all quarters, Eliana held a thirty-minute conversation with Citlali's mother about dinner preparations.

The morning of the party, Eliana grabbed a basket sitting outside Ixchel's garden and headed into the forest. She had spent enough time in the woods lately that she knew her way around. She knew the well-worn trail on the north end of the village led to the river for washing and bathing. She knew that the insects accrued more viciously the more you tried to swat them away. Like air and sweat and water, they were everywhere in the humid climate, and if she managed to pretend they weren't there long enough, she would eventually forget they were there at all.

She also knew where the most beautiful flowers were located, thanks to her tour through the area with Ixchel. About two hundred feet down the north trail, she encountered the river and turned upstream, removing her sandals to walk along the banks of the river until a patch of orange-and-blue orchids came into view. Their petals were coated in pollen at this time of year. When Ixchel first brought her here, Eliana had touched one and then put her fingers to her eyes, which made them burn so much she cried until Ixchel washed her eyes out with river water.

The orchids had no medicinal use, but they were beautiful and Ixchel admired them. This time, Eliana was more careful. She reached out and grasped the stem and, using a sharp rock she fished from the river, she cut two and placed them in her basket.

She walked back toward the trail, going straight through the trees instead of back along the river to the worn-down laundry area. She stepped slowly, enjoying the fresh mossy smells and the feel of the soft *lu'um* between her toes. She searched the ground for feathers. Most of the birds here were very small, so the women treasured large, brightly colored feathers. Eliana picked up a green one and wound through the trees absorbed in the search for more.

When she looked up again, she didn't know which direction the river lay. Straining, she heard no burble or rush of water. The forest was deeply silent.

When she first arrived, Eliana had been terrified of being alone in the jungle. Citlali had explained that there was nothing to be afraid of. When Eliana gave it some thought, she could not recall having seen any sign of predators in her many weeks in *Kakul*. Apart from the wild turkeys, a few birds, and the jaguar on the night of the sacrifice, she hadn't seen any other animals.

Now, rational or not, her fear of the forest returned. Swallowing hard, she fought down her panic and forced herself to stop spinning in circles. She looked up through the canopy and saw that the sun was rising to her right, in the direction of the ocean. She put the rising sun to her left and walked south, paying closer attention to her surroundings. After a few minutes that seemed to last an eternity, she came out of the trees onto a trail. It was narrower than the trail leading to the laundry spot.

Looking down the trail, she saw thick foliage and made out the shape of an archway overgrown with vines, hidden among the vegetation. Had her eyes not been trained to spot hidden structures, to piece shapes in the dirt into imagined artifacts in her mind, she might not have given it a second thought.

Now, she couldn't unsee it.

She had stumbled on a gateway to *Uchben Na*.

The reactive part of her mind screamed at her to turn tail and flee like a frightened child in the opposite direction. Back into the woods, for chrissakes, anywhere but *Uchben Na*.

Yet her logical mind, the archaeologist in her, was intrigued. She had never seen the stone city in the daylight, and the sun sparkled through the canopy so beautifully. What did those relief carvings on the inside of the archway depict? Who spent so much time and loving energy to carve them?

Stepping around a crumbling column supporting the deep arch, Eliana pushed aside a handful of vines. She saw a hand, a berobed set of legs, perhaps a sandaled pair of feet. As she pared back the vegetation, the full figure came into view. Instead of a face, the figure's head was covered in a circular mask—a helmet of some kind? And a floating ball hovered just over his shoulder.

Eliana's brow scrunched down. The vines and fungus growing on the wall made the relief difficult to see. Its outlines were weathered and worn. If she had the time and the tools she could cut away the vines, expose the relief, and carefully scrape off the moss until the picture became clear once more.

"Beautiful, isn't it?" said a deep voice in the language of *Kakul*.

Eliana jumped. Her heart slammed against her ribcage. Chief Dambu stood on the city side of the arch. The scabs were gone where Amon's ring had blasted him, and off-colored scars remained, marring the intricate designs of his tattoos. Eliana nodded.

He approached on sandaled feet that padded as quietly as a jungle cat, until he loomed over Eliana.

"What's in your basket?" he asked.

"Presents for…uh, for Ixchel," she said.

He grunted. He reached out to put his hand on her shoulder but hesitated and let his arm fall to his side. He circled around her, back to his original position. Beyond him, Eliana saw the cornice of a small, square structure with a flat open area atop it. Its stairs had been crushed by a toppled statue whose head had tumbled three feet from its body. Eliana could make out no features on the face of the statue either. Apart from a few cracks from the fall, its surface was perfectly smooth, and not because its edges had been worn down by the weather.

Dambu took a step closer. Eliana involuntarily stepped back.

"What..." she said, casting about for something, anything to talk about. "What are you doing here?"

"Searching for Xucha."

Had he lost his mind? Eliana didn't know how to respond.

"My ancestors carved these walls," Dambu said after a moment, reaching out and letting his fingers caress the vines and the reliefs hidden beneath them. "They built this city."

"What happened?" Eliana asked.

"They disobeyed Xucha. He brought a plague down and banished them from the city. He blotted out the sun and punished them for their actions." The chief exhaled heavily through his nose. "Like I was punished."

"You mean...your son?"

He dipped his chin sadly. "He is dead because of me." Then he pulled his shoulders back and gazed up at the underside of the arch.

She followed his gaze to where the vines ended and the arch curved across to its other side. At the center of the curve, a carved triangle pointed across the arch to two orbs of distinctly different sizes—a pyramid pointing at two moons.

"And yet," Dambu said, "*you* live."

Eliana glanced around. They were alone except for the soft buzz of insects and the occasional chirp of a bird.

"Ixchel is waiting for me," Eliana said. "I have to go."

The chief said nothing. He remained still as she hurried away from him, down the trail with *Uchben Na* at her back. Once, glancing over her shoulder, she saw him staring after her, his large form dwarfed by the ancient, partially concealed stone structure. When she looked back a second time, he was gone.

12
BREAKING AND ENTERING

AMON CALLED REUBEN back twice more, but the line went straight to voicemail.

He covered his face with his hands and fell limply from the chair to the cold concrete floor. He lay there and replayed in his mind the moment he reached for Eliana, the look of shock and awe on her face, and the feeling of slamming into unforgiving steel.

When his back couldn't handle the hard floor any longer, he sat up and glanced at the digital clock on the wall. It was midnight. When the digital numerals jumped from *12:00* to *12:01*, a curious idea struck him.

A desperate idea.

His eyes darted between the transponder prototype and the clock, and back again. It was a new day. He inhaled, holding his breath for a suspended moment. He let it out. It was a new day, and his desperate ideas were all he had left.

It only took a couple hours to connect the transponder to a small digital clock using a wire and electrical connector. It was even clunkier, this prototype extended from a prototype. He chuckled nervously. Streamlining their products had always been Reuben's specialty.

However, it took another three days of tireless developing, testing, and tweaking to build the software needed to activate the Hopper automatically and integrate it with the timer. The control unit was missing all sorts of protocols required for automation. He'd have to be very, very specific for it to work well, so he hard-coded the translocation destination into the forked version.

His new timer-activated prototype passed the basic tests his engineers had written for it, plus a few more he wrote himself to make sure the new timer features were working properly. He supposed that meant all systems checked out.

Looking at the screen, his vision swam. Whether the dizziness was a result of a lack of sleep or the fact that he only had a handful of protein bars left, he couldn't be sure. Maybe both.

There were risks, of course. No one was able to double check his work. He could have a blind spot in his tests. The clock could fry in the translocation. He could drop the transponder or step on it, or any number of other tiny casualties.

Not to mention real-world repercussions. He could be incarcerated for breaking into a NASA facility, even one he formerly had clearance to access. If they caught him or he didn't manage to find a way to isolate the meteorite sample for the translocation back into the lab—well, he kept himself from wandering too far down that road.

The phone buzzed.

"How you doing in there, Amon? Hungry yet?" Fowler asked in a crooning, sickly sweet voice when he answered the phone. She had developed a nasty new habit of checking in with him at 7 a.m. each morning. She was five minutes early today.

"I have enough organic, locally sourced smoothies to swim in. If I had a bathtub, I could turn my dream into a reality."

"You won't last forever," she said.

"Like hell I won't."

"You know we could blow down these steel-reinforced doors any time we want to, right?"

"Then why don't you? Does Montoya have bad aim?"

She repeatedly tried to talk him out of the lab. Amon's refusal had become the kind of familiar banter you repeated with friends who knew you always took the same stance on a certain political subject, a kind of game they played together, repeating it for different variations of the same outcome.

But at least she called. Truth be told, he looked forward to the brief moments of human contact, even those full of veiled threats and sarcasm. Lucas, who spent much effort early in Amon's isolation to maintain close contact, hadn't rung since Reuben spooked. Amon knew what it took to serve as CEO of Fisk Industries, how much time that role consumed. Especially when times were tough.

So he didn't begrudge Lucas. Times were the toughest they'd ever been. Amon wanted to be there for his employees, for the company, but his absence couldn't be helped. So he was glad it could be Lucas instead.

Amon waited for a while after Fowler disconnected the call to increase the chance that she wouldn't be in hearing range when he activated the Hopper. The high-pitched whine of the machine charging up wasn't unusual. Amon often spun it up to run diagnostic tests. But he was worried she would suspect the worst and didn't want to give her any advantage if it was within his power to prevent doing so. If she somehow divined that he'd gone *through* the Translocator this time, there was nothing to keep her from taking more drastic steps to end her siege.

Finally, Amon set the timer for forty-five minutes, hoping that gave him enough leeway. The Hopper came to life with a squeal, and he walked into the sphere, the transponder in his pocket already counting down.

He felt the familiar jolt, closed his eyes against the light, and when he opened them again he was standing in the middle of the east wing women's bathroom on the first floor of the NASA facility.

It smelled like antibacterial soap, the kind you could buy in bulk for $1.29 a gallon. He sniffed. NASA needed to stop being so cheap. Millions of dollars of research equipment lived in this building, and they refused to shell out for nice soap.

He chose the women's bathroom because there was less chance of crossing paths with another person when he reassembled. NASA had managed to attract some top female talent in recent years, a far cry from their male-dominated inception; Amon's company often competed with them to recruit talented young scientists. But apparently, the riveting field of meteorite studies didn't attract many females.

He peeked out the door of the bathroom and ducked back in when he saw shadows. Getting to the one woman he *did* want to cross paths with while he was here wouldn't be difficult—as long as he was careful. Audrey's office was located down the hall.

During his visit six months ago, when he mentioned in passing how a rare gem like she'd found would make a great ring to replace the one Eliana had lost, Audrey had given him the sample she took for her own personal collection. Not exactly in line with departmental policy. Amon had initially refused, but Audrey insisted. After all, they were friends. What was a fragment of space rock between friends?

He peeked out the door again. The white-tiled hall seemed empty now, quiet. He stepped quickly around the corner and almost ran into a security guard.

"Hello," Amon said, nodding to the man. He was skinny, young with a sharp chin. Amon moved briskly past him, trying to act like he belonged.

"Hey, wait a minute," the guard said. "Where's your badge?"

"Sorry?" Amon said, patting at his clothes like he was looking for it. "I must have dropped it. I'm a guest of Audrey Murphy. Her office is right there."

The guard's eyebrows scrunched into a V shape. "Wait a minute," he said. "You're Amon Fisk."

Amon sucked in his breath through his teeth. He nodded.

"I thought you were locked up in your basement or something."

"Heh. Can't believe everything you see on TV." Amon shrugged, backing away. "I really must be going."

"Well. I…"

Amon slipped into Audrey's office and leaned his back against the closed door.

"Amon!" Audrey said, standing from her desk, her frizzy red hair swinging in a loose ponytail. "I thought I heard your voice. How did you get in here?"

The guard banged on the door. "Ms. Murphy?"

"Help," Amon mouthed.

Amon sank into a chair facing her desk while Audrey pulled the door open and leaned her body against the door frame. "Hello, Barry. What can I do for you?"

"Is everything okay, ma'am?"

"Yes, fine."

"I need to see his guest badge."

"Oh. I think he dropped it on the floor. You have it there, don't you Amon?"

"That's right," he said, pretending to reach down under the chair. "I've got it."

Barry hesitated. "Well…"

"Thanks so much, sweetie." She closed the door in his face.

Barry waited for a moment. They saw his silhouette reach up to knock again through the frosted glass in the door. But he seemed to change his mind, and they listened to the sound of his footsteps carrying him away down the hall.

"What's up with them?" Amon asked.

"Ugh, I don't even want to talk about it. New agency policy. The extra cost for rent-a-cops is coming out of *our* budget. It's unbelievable. We can't even afford to buy nice soap for our staff bathrooms, but we have to pay for them."

"Audrey, I need your help," Amon said. His hand brushed over the awkward bulge of the transponder in his front pocket.

Audrey pushed her glasses up against the bridge of her nose with one finger and squinted at him. "Is this about Eliana?"

He nodded. "You remember that meteorite sample you gave me? For her new ring?"

"Of course."

"I suspect that's what caused the Translocator to malfunction. It interfered with the targeting process somehow. I've been trying for weeks to pin down her location, but I can't do it without another meteorite sample to test against."

"By golly, that's a wild theory."

"That's what Reuben said."

Her eyes widened. "Reuben," she breathed. "Is that why he contacted me and tried to visit? You should have told me."

"I know. I'm sorry. I didn't want to put you in a position where you had to cover for him."

"But…" she said. Her lips parted, and she glanced to the side, reasoning through the problem like the scientist she was. "Carbonados like the kind found in that meteorite are a result of shock metamorphism. The shockwaves and heat of a high velocity astronomical impact turns the carbon deposits in the meteorite into black diamonds. They're rare, and the polycrystalline structure is incredibly durable, but I don't see how they could interface with electronics."

Amon threw his hands up. "It's the only working theory I've got right now."

She pursed her lips. "You're lucky you came early. Almost no one else is here yet. Come on."

He followed Audrey to a familiar clean room made almost entirely of glass and metal. In the entryway, they donned latex gloves, face masks, slip-on covers for their shoes, and lab coats so that only their eyes were visible.

The dress code was protocol, Amon knew, but it was also better this way. If someone else walked in while they were looking for the meteorite they needed, there was less chance anyone would recognize him like the guard had.

In the next room, a checkerboard of fluorescent lights flickered on one by one, chasing the shadows away. The lab's floor plan was a rectangle divided into two equal squares. The far square housed six distinct testing areas separated by glass walls. In one, an integrated system of glove box isolators meant to reproduce atmospheric conditions found in outer space stood empty.

The near square, in which they stood, was used for storage. Sparse and spacious, glass-doored chrome cabinets lined the left wall, housing thousands of meteorite samples in individual hermetically sealed containers.

Audrey went straight to the corner, opened a bottom drawer, and carried a box the size of a small fish tank to a chrome table in the middle of the room.

"Here it is," Audrey said. "HB-Z404."

She removed an oblong rock with gloved hands and dragged over a microscope. The size of an overlarge football and pockmarked with small craters, the meteorite sample weighed nearly thirty pounds.

"This is the same one you took the original sample from?"

"That's right. It's truly an amazing find. Before we discovered HB-Z404, the only carbonados we'd found came from Brazil and parts of Africa. They dug this one up deep in the ice of Antarctica. It's ancient, and the meteorite was so big they only sent me a small chunk of it."

She scraped a few bits onto a glass slide and placed it under a nearby microscope. "Nothing unusual about the polycrystalline structure," she said. "The quality of the material is amazing, I've never seen another carbonado so clear. Usually, they look more like coal than the diamonds we're used to. But this one seems like a normal diamond to me. Are you sure it was her ring?"

"As sure as I can be. Is there any way to extract another sample without damaging the meteorite?"

"Oh, don't worry." Audrey's smile lit up her face. "We use very scientific methods here."

She removed a small hammer from a toolbox under the table and aimed a chisel at one corner of the football-shaped rock.

"Wait!" Amon said. "Is that a good idea?"

"Do you have a better one?"

"Not exactly."

She nodded and brought the hammer down. A chunk the size of ping-pong ball broke off.

"I guess you've done this a few times," Amon said.

"Do you think this is enough?"

"Should be. The stone in Eliana's ring was much smaller. I just need to make sure I have enough of the material because I won't be able to return again if I don't."

"Why not?"

"They don't know I'm gone."

Audrey's eyes widened. "You used the Translocator to get in here." It wasn't a question.

He couldn't remove the transponder from his pocket with the sterile lab attire over his clothes. If the clock on the wall was correct, he had ten minutes remaining.

"Oh," she said. "Oh no. How are you going to isolate the meteorite for the trip back?"

"I was hoping you had an idea."

She stared at him with wide eyes. "You're going to be the death of me, Amon."

After a moment spent rifling around on the far side of the lab, Audrey returned with a plastic bottle, a beaker, plastic wrap, and a rubber band. She poured a translucent, odorless liquid from the bottle into a wide-mouthed beaker. Then she picked up the meteorite sample and placed it into the liquid with a plop.

"Castor oil," Amon said. "Smart."

She covered the beaker with plastic wrap and then fitted the rubber band around it to hold the plastic wrap in place.

"It's not ideal," she said. "But it should do the trick of insulating the meteorite during the translocation."

"Thanks. I owe you one." Amon looked at a wall clock again. "I don't have much time."

"Let's get back to my office. People are in and out of here all day long."

Audrey returned the equipment and meteorite to its place. They took the lab coats, masks, and caps off and made their way back to Audrey's office. Liquid sloshed around in the wide beaker, which Amon carried with two hands like it was combustible. A liquid dielectric like castor oil, used to rapidly quench electrical discharges, would theoretically isolate the carbonado during the translocation. But he was still afraid it would backfire somehow. It wasn't like his luck was running high these days.

Within sight of Audrey's office, Barry the security guard came skidding around the corner. "Mr. Fisk," he said, fingering the Taser on his hip. "I'm afraid you'll have to come with me."

"What for?" Audrey said. "He's my guest."

The guard squinted at Amon. "Where's his badge?"

Amon swallowed. "I've got it right here," he lied. "One second." He made as if to step past Barry in the hall, but the young guard backed up and drew his Taser.

"What's that?" he asked, pointing to the beaker with his free hand. "Is that from the clean room?"

Amon charged, lowering his shoulder and driving it into Barry's chest. The sudden motion threw the guard off balance. His head glanced against the wall, and he staggered back. When he caught himself, he grunted and brought the Taser around in a semicircle. The weapon's tiny jaws crackled as it was activated mid-swing, aimed at the soft spot in Amon's neck. Amon cringed, clutching the beaker, but Audrey backhanded the Taser out of Barry's hands and sent it bouncing to the floor behind him.

Barry dove for it. Amon took two steps forward then stomped a foot down onto Barry's wrist. Barry screamed and clutched at Amon's ankle with his free hand. His fingers seized onto a handful of Amon's jeans.

Amon lunged away from him, stumbled, felt the waist of his pants as the hand gripping them yanked down. Oil sloshed around in the beaker, slipped out of the imperfect seal, and dripped onto the floor, onto Amon's jeans, onto Barry as they struggled. The oil greased Barry's hands as it fell, and his hold on Amon's jeans loosened until Amon was able to slip away.

Amon heard a half scream come from behind him. He turned back. Audrey held the Taser into Barry's side, her lips pressed together into a line, squinting and trying to pull her face away even as her arm pressed the Taser into him.

Amon didn't wait to say thank you. He turned again and sprinted down the hall, heading for the bathroom into which he'd arrived nearly forty-five minutes earlier. Two more security guards skidded around the corner from the opposite direction and blocked his way. One of them wore a black baseball cap screen printed with a white silhouette of a horse.

Amon took a left down a hall between them, turning his head rapidly from side to side in his search for an exit. He saw a small cracked window in an empty first-floor office, stepped inside, and locked the door behind him.

Setting the beaker down on a desk for a moment, he wiped his hands on his jeans and opened the cracked window as far as it would go, which was just barely enough for Amon to squeeze through. Taking the beaker back into his hands, he squirmed feet first through the window, the slippery beaker held against his stomach, trying not to jostle the carbonado too hard against the glass of the beaker. Nearly half the oil seemed to be all over his clothes, or the ground behind him.

He fell a few feet to the parking lot, twisting his ankle. At the same time, the other two guards burst noisily through the door of the office, screaming at him.

"Stop where you are!"

"Put the jar down!"

"That's an order!"

Oil spilled down one side of the beaker as he jostled it. Gripping the glass became a task for arms instead of hands. He stumbled forward onto the asphalt parking lot as the deafening pulse of helicopter blades crested the building and set down in front of him.

The rhythmic thrum of the blades penetrated his body. The security guards' screams became inaudible in the copter's windstorm. He edged farther toward the helicopter to get out of their reach as they squeezed themselves through the window.

Amon fumbled the transponder out of his pocket as the helicopter touched down. When he looked up, he saw a blurry white silhouette of a horse's head—like a chess knight—printed on the tail, the same as the guard's cap. Fowler and Montoya jumped to the ground with their handguns drawn.

"You're surrounded, Fisk!" Fowler yelled. "Nowhere to go now."

Amon didn't say anything. His eyes remained fixed on the transponder's timer. Ten seconds remaining. The helicopter blades slowed down. Montoya held out his pistol and stepped forward. The timer reached zero. It stopped.

Nothing happened.

Amon drew in a sharp breath, and when he looked up he was gazing down the barrel of Montoya's gun.

13
THE LEGEND OF KY AND KAL

ELIANA RAN BACK to her hut as fast as her feet would carry her. A lovely blue feather blew out of her basket. She did not even consider turning back for it. At last, she stumbled into her shelter and collapsed on her bed, clutching the basket in her lap, her chest heaving, her heart pounding, still scared but feeling more secure in the humid shade of her hut.

The encounter with the chief had shaken her to the core. There were so many unanswered questions running through her mind. She feared asking them would cause a sudden end to her freedom, to her life. Would she fall ill like the boy, Tilak? Would the gods punish her, too?

She needed allies now more than ever. Eliana decided to go ahead with her original plan in spite of her fears. When she caught her breath, Eliana arranged the orchids she had collected. Despite the loss of a few, she had enough for a small bouquet. Only three of the half-dozen feathers she had gathered survived the journey. She wanted to give them away. Gifts, even simple ones, would be appreciated and remembered.

Ixchel was not in her hut when Eliana arrived, so she left the orchids on the adobe porch at the foot of the front door. The neighbors who saw her leave them would tell Ixchel whom they were from.

"She loves those," someone said. Eliana spun. Rakulo stood two feet behind her. He had a shy smile on his face.

"Oh, hello," Eliana said. "I didn't know you were standing there." She walked around him, headed back to her hut. He followed, jogging to catch up and match her pace. Eliana fought down a smile.

"'A warrior is silent in life and death,'" Rakulo said.

"What does *that* mean?"

"It's something my father says. It is a matter of honor to move quietly and to say little. He says it's a sign of strength."

Eliana didn't have a word for creepy, so she didn't say anything.

The village was still waking up. People were in their homes getting ready for the big gathering that day. When they reached Eliana's hut at the edge of the village, no one could be seen lingering nearby.

Eliana noticed Rakulo fidgeting. He seemed slightly embarrassed to be alone with her.

"Wait here a moment," she said, ducking inside to retrieve the feathers. She handed Rakulo the small orange one and tucked the other two into her shirt.

"For you," she said.

"Thanks," Rakulo said. "Um…Will you be at the bonfire tonight?"

"Of course. I spent the last week helping prepare for it. I wouldn't miss it."

He nodded. "All right. See you later then."

As he turned to go, Eliana had an idea. The uneasy feeling from her encounter with the chief remained, but perhaps this was her opportunity to get some of her questions answered after all.

"Rakulo?" she said as he turned. "Do you want to walk to the beach with me?"

He stopped, hesitated, turned back to her. "Sure."

They each picked up a bundle of wood kindling from a pile that needed to be brought down to the beach. When they were alone again on the trail, Eliana asked, "Why does your father hate me?"

"He doesn't hate you."

"It sure seems like he does."

Rakulo adjusted the load of wood in his arms as he considered his answer. At a bend in the trail, he slowed down and said, "A long time ago, some people in *Kakul* started questioning the old ways. They didn't want to feed the gods anymore. But when they refused to participate in the ceremony, people started getting very sick."

"Like Tilak got sick?"

"Yes."

Eliana asked, "Did all the ones who questioned the old ways get sick?"

"Not always. Their brother or child might become sick instead. Someone in their family."

Eliana clenched her jaw. "As punishment."

Rakulo nodded.

"I'm so sorry."

He wiped his eyes discretely on the back of his arm and managed to stem the flood of tears that threatened to overwhelm him. They took another bend in the road. Rakulo looked up and down the trail and took a breath before continuing.

"After the previous chief—the one before my father—died of the sickness, the elder shamans convinced our people to return to the old ways. They performed the ceremony during the next cycle of the moons. And when the sickness passed, my father made peace with the shamans, and they elected him chief."

"How long ago was this?"

"Many moons. I was a child."

Eliana thought, *You still are*. She asked instead, "Have many fallen ill since then?"

"Some. But until Tilak, it had been a while."

"What are the shamans doing about it?" she asked.

"There aren't any left. One died three moons past in a turkey hunting accident. Another drowned. Another died in his sleep. The last...well, you saw what happened to him."

The memory of Chief Dambu stripping the shaman of his headdress and clothes and slopping purple paint onto him as he gasped for breath returned to her mind's eye, the memories' details cemented by their association with simultaneous terror and joy. When she realized she had stopped walking, Eliana shook her head and picked up her pace again.

After a moment of reflection, she asked, "Why did the shamans not recruit young ones to take their place when they were gone?"

"All of the young men want to be warriors like my father. They take his words to heart."

"And the young women?"

"They want to be warriors, too," he said with a chuckle. "Like Citlali."

"She is fierce," Eliana agreed. "And silent. I guess that makes sense." The new information about Citlali surprised her and made her feel guilty at the same time. Eliana knew that she had been so busy learning *from* the girl that she had not taken much time to learn *about* her. "What about the other girls?" she asked.

"They want to be healers, like my mother, or get pregnant and have babies as a…safeguard against the necessities. Those old enough to have seen their cousins and siblings fall ill know the toll it takes on our village."

It was starting to come together now for Eliana, the unspoken logic of the midnight sacrifices. "So that's why your father, instead of a shaman, led the ceremony?"

"Yes. There is no one else."

They had reached the beach now. Eliana dumped her bundle of kindling next to a large pit that had been dug for the bonfire.

"Will you be chief one day, like Dambu?"

Rakulo dropped his bundle of kindling next to hers then walked toward where the translucent lavender waves lapped gently against the shore. He bent and gathered a fistful of sand and chucked it at the horizon. A gust of wind caught the tiny grains and scattered them as they fell.

"I don't want to be chief," he said.

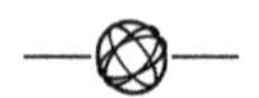

Eliana and Rakulo made three more trips to gather wood. By their second trip, the trail was crowded with people making their way down to the beach with their families.

When Eliana ran into Citlali, she withdrew the two remaining feathers from her tunic, a large pink one with a rounded edge, and a comb-edged royal-blue-and-black one. Citlali's eyes lit up as Eliana tied them into her hair. It pleased her immensely when the boys complimented Citlali over the course of the afternoon. Even more so, when the other girls looked jealously at Eliana's gifts.

By the time the sun began to set, the bonfire had been built up to a fierce blaze. Eliana sipped from a cup of sweet wine where she sat on a tree trunk at the back of many rows of logs arranged theater style around the fire. The event reminded her of afternoon picnics and barbecues back home, a time of socializing and laughter. Sitting apart, she grew melancholy with nostalgia.

Rakulo played throwing games with the other young teenagers his age. She caught him looking in her direction a few times.

Dambu mingled among the crowd, greeting friends and thanking them for coming. He had not been involved in the preparations, yet, as chief, he was the host of this event. He welcomed everyone. He even acknowledged Eliana and the work she did helping them put it together, giving no hint of their conversation that morning.

At full dark, with the two moons waxing to a synchronous full showing overhead, Ixchel gathered the children in a cleared area before the fire. The older adults slowly filtered into the rows of logs, choosing seats. The younger adults gathered at the back and stood when there were no more logs on which to sit.

The crowd pressed in tightly to hear Chief Dambu as he took the impromptu stage. Tongues of orange flame licked the inky purple sky. His great feathered headdress—the headdress that had once belonged to an elder shaman—fanned out over his broad shoulders and chest, which had been painted blue and green, augmenting his tattoos into more sinuous forms that crawled across his neck and face. The scars on his chest were shiny and pale in the firelight. He put his hands over his heart then raised them toward the night sky, touching the thumb and forefinger of each hand together. The crowd mimicked his gesture.

A-okay. Eliana shivered.

Dambu drew the obsidian knife from his belt. "May Xucha accept our offering," he said, his deep baritone carrying out over the quiet crowd. "Protect us, keep our children in good health, and bless us with a plentiful harvest for the season."

He beckoned with his free hand, and Rakulo reluctantly rose from his seat. The painted designs on Rakulo's arms and chest made him look like a modest imitation of the chief.

When he reached his father's side, Rakulo turned to face the crowd. Chief Dambu grasped his son's wrist with one hand. Pulling his arm out, empty palm facing up, Dambu exposed the many lines of scars along Rakulo's forearm. He drew the obsidian knife across Rakulo's forearm, opening a fresh wound. Rakulo bore it in silence, clenching his jaw. Then Dambu sheathed the knife and caught the dripping blood in a bowl held below the open cut. Eliana cringed.

"For Xucha!" Dambu cried out, his eyes bulging in his head. He dipped his fingers in the bowl of blood and drew a circle on each of Rakulo's cheeks. He cast the rest of the blood into the fire with a bloodthirsty cry. People held their hands up in the A-okay sign and stomped their feet until the ground shook.

Dambu wrapped Rakulo's arm with cloth and sent him back to his mother's side. Ixchel embraced him and rubbed his back. Citlali reached over and patted his leg. Rakulo looked nauseous, but he put on a brave face as his blood soaked the wrapping on his arm.

"Let the storytelling begin," Dambu intoned. He made his way to the back of the crowd, where he stood with his arms crossed and melted into the shadows.

The first performer who took the stage wore a wooden mask painted with an image of a fanged snake. He threw a handful of herbs on the fire, and the flames turned a vibrant blue.

Snake spun a yarn about the serpent god, Xucha, who cracked open the sky with his split tongue and let the other gods in. Together, they fashioned the world from clay and stone, filled it with water, covered it with trees, brought forth animals to inhabit the jungle, and, as their final act, formed man out of clay. When the world was complete, Xucha wrapped his sinuous body around the world and squeezed the sky shut. But he squeezed too tight, and the sky turned a bruised purple as a result. The sky was broken, and even the gods were stuck here, and no one could go back through again.

Snake cast his hand out behind him, and the flames glowed a bright lavender.

Children oohed and ahhed in the front row. Adults near Eliana smiled at the familiar tricks.

Snake stepped back. Bird took his place. His mask, too, was carved of wood and painted in bright colors, but a sharp beak extended from the nose.

Bird told a story of the deluge, another classic myth. Eliana recognized the permutation: The world flooded, taking the evil sinners with it, and the *Kakuli* people survived by building a gigantic ark and floating around the world, waiting for the water to recede. Their voyage was not peaceful. They sent birds to find land, but the birds were eaten by a sea monster. The monster attacked their boat, and many died defending it. Bird pulled a stick from the fire and brandished it like a sword as he acted out the battle between the captain of the ark, Kakul himself, and the beast. Kakul jumped from the boat into the sea to wrestle with the monster and slayed the beast by plunging a knife into the soft spot in its throat. When Kakul made it back to the ark, cold and wet but victorious, they sent out another bird, who helped them find their way to land, where Kakul and his family began to build their lives anew.

Bird receded into the background, and Jaguar sauntered forward.

"When this world was born," he growled, pointing up, "the beautiful purple sky above us was empty except for clouds in the day, stars at night, and the smoky campfires of our people, who lived in *Uchben Na*.

"It was a peaceful city. The people led a simple life. They farmed the land and fished the sea. They ascended the temple steps to the observatory's open dome to study the stars. They passed the time by painting beautiful art on the walls of the city, weaving fine cloth, and telling stories—much like we do this night in remembrance."

Eliana, who had been watching the children fidget in their seats, tuned in to the story again. Unlike the stories that came before, this one was unfamiliar to her and extraordinarily detailed. She wondered how much of it was truth, how much legend, and where the blurred line between them might be drawn.

"The violent events of the world's creation and the flood were long behind them. But one day, during the Summer Solstice Festival, blazing rocks rained fiery death out of the sky and laid waste to that great city. The world shook, and our people fled.

"For years, a blanket of gray clouds hung low over the land, and people lived off the sea, an endless diet of fish. With the sun blotted out, no maize grew. The waves of the ocean crashed on the shores, sometimes as tall as the trees. The ground heaved and shuddered.

"After wandering the coast for another place to settle, and finding none where the clouds did not cover the sky, two warrior twins, Ky and Kal, led the folk of the White Cliffs back to their ruined city. Fearing that the gods had been angry at them for building their cities of stone and forgetting the old ways, they settled outside of *Uchben Na* and named the village *Kakul* after the great ark builder of legend. Kal himself, having some skill with the land, cleared the overgrown fields and planted maize seeds he had kept safe.

"He waited and prayed. Despite his offerings of gems and cloth, of bone and blood, no crops grew. The clouds continued to blot out the sun, and the groundwater was poison to their plants.

"In a dream, Xucha came to Ky in the form of a jaguar, showing him how he could bring life to *Kakul* by going into the old city. So Ky went into *Uchben Na* and prostrated himself before Xucha on the summit of the great moon temple. He meditated there for three weeks, taking no food and only a cup of water each day. He waited for a sign from the gods, some hint that they might end the dark days and return light and life to the world.

"At the end of three weeks, when Ky had grown thin, Xucha spoke to him. He told Ky that prayer was not enough. Instead, Ky must sacrifice himself and offer his lifeblood to the gods."

The person in the seat next to her brushed Eliana's arm. She startled. Coming back to herself, she realized that her breath came in short gasps. She glanced behind her at where Chief Dambu had been standing, but he was nowhere in sight. She wanted to run, but she held her seat, her palms sweaty.

"When Kal found out that Ky wanted to cut his own heart out, he cried out in anguish and threw himself at his beloved brother's feet, offering himself in his place.

"It was worse than he believed. Xucha not only wanted Ky to offer his heart, but he wanted Kal to hold the dark knife himself—" Jaguar pulled a sharp stone from his belt, "—making Kal the first shaman since the day *Uchben Na* was abandoned."

Jaguar bowed his head and held out his free hand with his palm up. He gripped the obsidian blade and pulled away in a single, smooth motion, opening his palm with a long, shallow cut. Jaguar passed his bloody hand over the heads of the children, who raised their faces and held out their hands to receive the dark liquid. They rubbed it into their faces and arms, ecstatic. The adults murmured their approval.

Eliana put her hand over her mouth and masked a silent scream. *This is wrong,* she thought. *This is all wrong.*

"Ky instructed his brother to make himself a mask with Xucha's face on it. Then, at midnight, they made their way to the top of the temple. The whole village was there—their very livelihood at stake. A massive stone had been placed on the summit of the temple, perfectly square with a bulge in the middle. No one knew how it got there, but Ky lay down on his back and opened his arms to receive the blessing of the gods.

"Kal closed his eyes tight and plunged the knife into his brother. His aim was bad, and the blade bit into his brother's shoulder. Crying out, he pulled the knife up and plunged it down again, straight into his brother's chest. He drew the blade across, pulled out Ky's heart, and offered it to the gods.

"But nothing happened. Thinking that he had ruined the sacrifice with his bad aim, and determined not to let his twin brother die in vain, Kal set his brother's body aside, lay on the wet stone himself, and cut his own heart out. He offered that to the gods, and then his body went still. His heart fell from his hands, bounced down the temple steps, and landed in the courtyard, splashing the people with his blood.

"For a single moment, all was silent. No one dared to touch Kal's warm heart on the ground.

"Slowly, a cool breeze picked up. No one had felt a breeze since the day of the calamity. This breeze was refreshing. It smelled of the sea. The wind moved faster,

faster, faster. *Junrakan* lifted the hearts and bodies of Ky and Kal into the sky then blew the clouds away.

"Where before, a deep-purple expanse stretched across the night sky decorated only by stars, now there were two moons, casting a light as bright as day on the stones of *Uchben Na*. The large moon had a chunk taken out of its shoulder. Our people named it Ky. The loyal, smaller, bloodied moon that traveled always near him they named Kal."

Jaguar pointed at the two moons waxing toward full in the sky as he named them.

"The next morning, the sun came up, the corn grew tall, the water ran pure. Our people celebrated. To this day, we honor their sacrifice with one of our own, in sight of the gods, when the eyes of Ky and Kal are open."

Eliana followed the gaze of the bloody-faced children. The moons would both be full, for the second time since she had arrived, in a matter of days.

How had she been so foolish as to come to trust these people? Surely, when the time came, she would be the first to be stretched over the stone. They had nearly done it once. What would stop them from doing it again?

She stood and left the gathering, bumping knees with those seated near her as she squeezed out of the row. When she reached the edge of the pressing crowd, she didn't try to contain her anxiety. She let it stretch its legs as she stretched hers, running down the beach, fast and away. She pumped her arms, paying no attention to the sand at her feet. She knew the way.

When she reached the place where she had carved Amon's name in the sand, she fell atop the last letter, blurring it. She heaved ragged breaths, drawing in the balmy night air and feeling grains of sand in her mouth. Rivers of sweat poured down her body, yet she shivered.

Her fingers caressed the black diamond while she caught her breath. It had bounced out of her tunic in the run. She stroked the ring with wet, sandy fingers, holding in her mind the image of her husband. She missed him so bad it felt like a physical ache.

She had to face it. Amon wasn't coming. She was on her own. It felt like she had been here for years, though it had only been a few months if her count was right. The weather, a continuous strangling heat, gave no sign of ebbing. Who knew how long she had really been on this lost planet?

Most likely, Amon had no idea where she was. He would have come for her by now if he did. Eliana had no idea, not really, where in the universe she had ended up after she got sucked through the Translocator. Gazing up at the foreign sky, she felt a pang of homesickness in her chest. What she would give to see the shape of the Big Dipper again, or the face in Earth's moon!

As she stared up, searching for answers among foreign constellations, she noticed a soft red glow coming from behind her.

Carefully, she crept to the edge of the trees where the beach butted up against the jungle in undulating dunes. She kept her body low, nestled in the curve of the sand, her face hidden by the fractal leaves of low bushes.

When she got close enough to see through the bushes, she noticed something she had never seen before: a small game trail a few yards into the dense jungle.

On the trail, two men stood facing each other. One was huge, bare-chested, tattooed, with a thick ring through the septum of his nose. The other was taller but slimmer, dressed more like a man on earth than a *Kakuli*, with all his limbs and skin covered by his clothes. Black clothes.

Eliana recognized the big man as Chief Dambu. He had removed the headdress he wore at the storytelling. But in the dim glow of the red light, it was hard to mistake him.

The other man was a few inches taller than the chief. The smooth, shiny fibers he wore appeared to be synthetic. His hands were covered with gloves. His head was hidden completely by a helmet, like a motorcycle helmet or an astronaut's helmet, but made of a seamless piece of glass.

Eliana stifled her own gasp of shock as she recognized him from the sacrifice ceremony: the god they called Xucha.

Painted on the front of his helmet was the open mouth of a snake like the paintings on the storytellers' masks—but more detailed, more realistic than an artist's depiction. And it was strange, because it seemed to move in sync with the voice coming from the man, the snake's maw gaping and closing, its fangs protruding from the glass, shifting, expressing itself.

The red light came from a metal orb, about two feet in diameter, which hovered above and slightly behind the helmeted man's left shoulder. It emitted a low humming sound like a small engine.

Eliana trembled and pressed her body deeper into the sand dune, rustling the leaves that served as her cover. The two glanced her way. She exhaled softly.

They looked away and spoke again in low tones, apparently unaware of her presence.

"Please," Dambu said, "it is not his time."

Xucha's voice came out garbled like it had been chewed by metallic teeth. "That is not for you to decide."

"I did what you asked. She lives among us. Why is she still unsuitable?"

"She has another purpose."

Dambu clenched his fists.

"Need I remind you the price you paid for disobeying me?" Xucha asked. The tongue of the snake flickered.

Dambu cast his eyes down.

Xucha said, "The child's life will be a great boon for the gods. Your predecessor understood these things. He was grateful for his role."

Perhaps it was the red glow, but Dambu seemed to gaze up at the helmeted man with haunted, hate-filled eyes. "The last chief was right," he said. "There is no end to it. Each cycle, a younger one is chosen. This time, a child? I won't do it."

"You must, and you will."

Dambu's nostrils puffed out with his breath like a gored bull staring down the matador.

"No," he said.

Xucha made a fist, and Dambu cried out, the veins in his neck bulging, his jaw clenching. Dambu fell to his knees and writhed on the ground in agony. Eventually, Xucha relaxed his fist. Dambu lay panting on the forest floor. When he pushed himself to his feet again, Dambu said, "Praise Xucha," then turned and staggered into the night.

The helmeted man's voice lashed out in anger, but the sound cut out abruptly. He turned around and walked into the trees in the other direction. The orb mirrored his movements precisely as it floated along several feet behind him. His form blurred and slowly vanished from the feet up. The glowing orb finally floated behind a copse of trees and left Eliana in darkness.

When man and god were gone, Eliana let out an explosive breath, her whole body shuddering with tremors. Her mind raced. The moving snake face on the man's helmet, the floating orb of light... how was it possible that it could exist right next door to pole-and-thatch houses, obsidian knives, and blood worship?

Something rustled the branches mere feet from Eliana's hiding place. She slid deeper into the sand as a large shadow passed in front of the moon.

14
THE BLAST DOOR

"GET ON THE ground," Montoya said as he advanced. He held the pistol out steadily. *Semper Fi* was tattooed on the inside of his left forearm. "Slowly."

Amon fumbled the beaker in the crook of his arm like a wet football, trying to get both hands out to examine the transponder.

"I said drop it!"

"Are you kidding?" Amon said, stalling for time as he untangled the wires leading into the exposed circuit board of the digital clock display. "This is volatile material, man! If I drop it, we all go kablooey."

Montoya regripped his pistol. A bead of sweat tracked down the ridge of his nose. His eyes darted toward Fowler.

The clock dropped when Amon freed the tangle of wires from the grips of their neighbors. He saw that one of the wire connectors, a small comb-like rectangle with metal pins, had come undone, possibly as he'd removed it from his pocket. He snapped it back into place with a thumb and forefinger.

"He's bluffing!" Fowler said between her teeth. "Cuff him already."

Butterflies seized Amon's stomach, and the beaker slipped through his grasp. Glass shattered. Oil sloshed over his shoes.

Amon's head snapped up. The curved bank of monitors of the Hopper's control unit were visible through overlapping bands of blue-green alloy. A vast roar of echoing silence filled the large room, an intense contrast to the furor of shouting and thrumming helicopter blades he'd left behind. Once again, Amon found himself alone in his lab.

Broken glass and oil covered the translocation platform. After some searching, he found the meteorite sample, which had been washed over the side of the platform after the beaker burst.

He cleaned the meteorite off in the kitchenette sink, set it down to dry, then checked the computer. The internal teleconference line didn't record call history, but out of habit, he pulled up the anonymized chat program. To his surprise, a message from Reuben waited for him. It read:

> *BRING ME IN.*

Amon blinked. He double checked the timestamp on the message. It had come in at five that morning, nearly two hours before he'd translocated into the NASA facility to go after the meteorite.

His gut clenched. Someone had spooked Reuben and then tipped off Fowler and Montoya. How could he be certain this wasn't another ruse? He typed back,

> *PROVE IT'S YOU.*

While Amon waited for a response, he ransacked the lab, hedging against a worst-case scenario.

Say it wasn't Reuben. Or if it was Reuben, say he was being coerced into sending those messages. If an impersonator made it into the lab, Amon would have to be ready for whatever happened next.

The lab didn't contain any weapons, however. At least not if you didn't count the glass shards littering the platform.

So Amon made the best out of what he had available. Instead of cleaning up the oil and glass, he swept it onto the ramp leading down from the platform, making it slick and sharp. Then he cranked the brightness of the wall monitors up until they were a solid white and pointed all the other table lamps in the direction of the platform. Finally, he grabbed two fire extinguishers and set them by the computer.

This was a particle physics lab, not an armory.

He could get the jump on two, maybe three, people with the fire extinguishers, the bright lights, and the oil-slicked ramp covered in broken glass. If they managed to sneak through more than three—and the translocation platform, built for industrial use, could surely accommodate more—they'd overwhelm him.

Another message from Reuben waited for him on the computer.

> *WHO DO YOU THINK YOU'RE TALKING TO? I'M NOT SOME OLD PUTZ. AND YOUR TRANSPONDER DESIGNS ARE SLOPPY.*

Amon smiled. It was Reuben dictating the messages, all right. Whether he was being coerced remained to be seen.

If Amon really was going to go through after Eliana, he needed someone in the lab to man the Hopper while he was gone. He couldn't use the timer trick, for the search could take days, even weeks.

So he needed someone to activate the Hopper to bring him and Eliana back through once he gave the signal using the transponder. But more importantly, he needed Reuben to protect the Hopper while he was gone and make sure the way back to Earth stayed open for them.

He wrote to Reuben again:

> *OK. YOU KNOW WHAT TO DO. MESSAGE WHEN CLEAR.*

Then Fowler rang in on the internal teleconference line.

"Ah, Ms. Fowler," Amon said. "How was your flight?"

"Cut the crap, Amon. You broke into NASA. You stole from a federal facility." Fowler's self-righteousness rang out in her voice, but to Amon it sounded thin and harried.

"I didn't break into anything," Amon said. "Honest."

"I've had enough of this."

"Who tipped you off?" Amon said, switching subjects.

Silence on the other end of the line.

"You knew I was down there," he badgered her. "Who told you?"

She answered indirectly. "You're a fugitive now. As soon as the judge calls me with the warrant—"

"Bullshit! We both know you're not really FBI agents, so give up the charade."

Her voice turned icy. "Either way, we're blowing this door off its hinges and putting an end to this foolishness once and for all."

"Just so you know, blast doors have no hinges. But more importantly, if you try to blow through a ten-ton blast door with brute force, you'll kill us all. Except me. I'll be fine. That's what the blast door is for."

"Smartass," Fowler said before she slammed down the receiver.

Amon's grin faded as he sagged over the desk. Fighting a war on two fronts was starting to take its toll. Messing with Fowler's head wouldn't work for much longer. Part of Amon was surprised he'd lasted this long without someone trying to force their way into the lab. He supposed one crazed scientist wasn't worth the effort.

A new notification blinked across the computer screen.

> *READY.*

Amon turned the brightness of the walls up to max and clutched the fire extinguisher to his body. Then he keyed up the Hopper, homed in on Reuben's transponder, and translocated Reuben into the lab.

"*Oy gevalt*," Reuben said when he appeared, clutching his head. "Do you mind, with the lights?"

The fire extinguisher slipped from Amon's fingers and hit the floor with a metallic rattle. He ran forward, crunching glass underfoot without concern, and embraced Reuben in a bear hug.

Reuben squirmed under Amon's grip. "Easy there, kid."

Amon laughed. "It's so good to see you."

"You're hurting me," he complained.

"Sorry! Sorry. I'm just so glad to see you."

Reuben smiled and shook his head. "I'm sorry I bailed on you."

"It's not your fault. Forget it."

Reuben walked Amon through the troubles he'd had over the past several weeks. He told Amon about his chats with Audrey. He shared what it was like to be tailed by a private detective, who appeared shortly after he was rejected by NASA's security system. Finally, he relayed the experience of the assault. "One day, I come home, and a man in a black ski mask is waiting for me. I knew they'd been trailing me, but I thought they were just keeping tabs. I hadn't actually done anything illegal yet, you understand. But he beat the tar out of me. Threatened me. I've never been more scared in my life."

"I don't blame you."

Amon inspected Reuben's face, the three stitches on his forehead, and yellowish-brown swollen flesh around his eye.

"You're sure it was a private detective following you?" Amon said. "Not an FBI agent?"

"I can't be sure of anything."

"And the guy who attacked you?"

"If he was FBI, we're all doomed. I don't know. Hard to tell when a fella is covered in black from head to foot, but I guess he could have been military. Had the build and the posture for it, not to mention the anger. You know the type?"

The image of Montoya pointing a pistol at him remained fresh in his mind. "I do," Amon said.

Reuben explained how he flew Charlie out west and got him a room at Miriam Ben-Gurion, a Jewish assisted-living facility in Beverly Hills. He also put a will in place so that Charlie would be well-taken care of if anything happened that might prevent Reuben from paying the bills.

"His Alzheimer's is getting worse," Reuben said while Amon made them instant coffee in the kitchenette. "We used to be so close. Now when we talk on the phone or if I go to visit him, most of the time he doesn't even remember my name. What kind of quality of life does a person have at that point? But you and Eliana, you're both young. And if she really is alive out there somewhere, I owe it to you both to help find her. Besides, I feel responsible for her disappearance. I helped build the Hopper. I keep thinking, what if it was Charlie, you know? I couldn't live knowing I had a chance to help and didn't."

"I'm glad to have you back," Amon said. "There's a lot of work to do. We don't have the resources between us to spend any more time trying to figure out what went wrong. If the meteorite sample works, and I suspect it will, we have to focus on recreating Eliana's translocation exactly, so that I can follow the same vector she took wherever it leads. I'll bring the transponder. As soon as I activate it on that end and you receive the signal, you can bring us home."

"Is that safe? You don't know what's on the other side."

"We'll take precautions," Amon said.

Reuben nodded, stroking his chin. "It's going to take time. But it's doable."

"I don't think we have much time."

While they were looking for something heavy with which to break the meteorite sample into pieces, a thin vibrating noise rose into the air.

"Is that the Hopper?" Reuben asked.

Amon, finely attuned to every sound in his personal bunker, turned to face the steel blast door that blocked the only entrance and exit.

"No," he said. "Fowler and Montoya are drilling into the blast door."

15
SURVIVAL KIT

CALLOUSED FINGERS BRUSHED Eliana's neck. She screamed and rolled to the side. The soft sand of the dune in which she hid shifted beneath her. She staggered to her feet, supporting herself with her hands and knees. A vine hidden in the dune tangled her foot when she tried to run. She plowed face-first into the sand.

"Eliana?"

She scrabbled back, kicking up dust.

"It's me! Eliana, it's me."

She looked up into the face of Rakulo. She coughed on a mouthful of sand. Fine grains clung to her clammy skin.

"Oh my god," she said. "You scared me!"

"Are you okay? What were you doing in there?"

Without thinking, Eliana opened her mouth to tell Rakulo everything, but closed her mouth before the words escaped. She shook her head and walked toward the water.

She stopped next to the remnants of Amon's name where it had been carved into the beach, trying with an effort of willpower to gather a sense of calm into herself, to rediscover her ability to reason.

Rakulo stood nearby, unconsciously fingering the dark-stained wrapping on his forearm while Eliana got control of herself again.

In the end, she decided that despite the honesty she sensed in her earlier conversation with Rakulo, his family ties were too complicated to trust him with what she had just witnessed.

"I left a rock there in the dune. To draw this," she said, gesturing to Amon's name.

"Where is the rock?"

"Couldn't find it."

A moment passed. Rakulo asked, "What does the drawing mean?"

"It's my husband's name," she said. "Amon."

"Where is he?"

"I don't know."

Eliana walked back toward the bonfire. Rakulo journeyed with her in silence.

When they reached the crowd, Eliana saw that the storytelling had ended. However, the party was just getting underway. A crowd of adults danced near the dying fire, took long swigs from water skins filled with liquor, and sang into the night.

Rakulo stumbled into Eliana's side. "Whoa!" she cried. "Easy."

He nodded. His skin looked pale in the firelight.

"I'm pretty tired, too," Eliana said. "How about we make our way back up to the village?"

She found a cup of water for Rakulo. He drained it, and then they walked back up to the village together, matching pace with the older folks who led their children home to put them to bed.

Instead of going to sleep when she and Rakulo parted, Eliana gathered her few belongings in the darkness of her hut and stayed awake while she waited for the late-night revelers to drink the last of the alcohol and finally turn in. She jumped at every snapping twig, every rustle of leaves outside of her door. When everyone seemed to be asleep and the party was over, Eliana set out to raid the outbuildings of the people of *Kakul*.

Before dawn, she slipped through several of the breezy pole-and-thatch dwellings used as pantries, never making a sound. She scooped up a handful of dried mangos, lifted some tree nuts, and stacked up pieces of salted fish. An astute cook might notice the food was missing, but possibly not for days, and none would suffer for what she took.

As she returned to her hut burdened with her bounty, the village lay quiet save for the constant buzz of insects. *It was funny,* Eliana reflected, *how one managed to tune out the regular noises of any place after a certain amount of time spent there.* The calls of songbirds from the trees and the low-hanging cloud of tiny insects had become part of the background noise of life—neither noticed nor noticeable. Unless, as now, she directed her senses toward those sounds.

The whole time she'd been in *Kakul,* a constant feeling of unease had plagued her. At first, she had chalked it up to two close encounters with death. Anyone would feel uneasy after that. The mysteries of the native religion also puzzled her. She knew that many cultures practiced ritual sacrifice—the Vikings, the ancient Hindus, the Aztecs, and the brilliant Mayans. As an archaeologist, perhaps she had been more accepting than others might have been after seeing it firsthand. But sacrifice wasn't the whole story either.

As she filled her rucksack with food and her only change of clothes, she finally realized what it was: a distinct lack of wildlife. Sure, there were the insects, the perpetual swarms of them; and the bird calls she heard in the forest, though she rarely glimpsed more than flits of color through the canopy. And there were the wild turkey-like birds, which the men hunted and which served as a staple of the *Kakuli* diet.

But she had seen no lizards or snakes, no monkeys, no wild boars, no ferrets, no foxes. She had not caught sight of a single cow, sheep, or horse. And though it was not unusual for an established human civilization to forego domesticating their animals, it was unsettling that she had not seen a single dog or cat, indeed no pets of any kind. And apart from Xucha when he morphed into a jaguar—which Eliana was still not certain was not just the culminating vision in a nightmarish hallucinogenic experience—no predators.

She shivered. It was so...un*real*. What kind of human population existed without a single competing predator nearby? No wonder the village women ventured into the jungle alone, unafraid and unconcerned. The lack of wildlife seemed like the shadow of some greater mystery, made even more unsettling by the presence of such totems in their mythology.

The foul play she had seen between Dambu and the mysterious Xucha this evening existed on yet a higher plain of horror. The ease with which Xucha brought Dambu to his knees without laying a hand on him made her quake with fear. Not a hallucination, Eliana was certain, but high technology. She thought of Earth equivalents—long-distance and close-range electroshock weapons, remote controls of various sorts. Practically magic compared to the technology available to the natives of *Kakul*.

Terrifying, all-powerful, blood-thirsty devil magic.

She slung her rucksack over her shoulders. Awkward to carry, but it was the best she could do on short notice. She surveyed the hut one last time.

She barely made it to the edge of the village before Rakulo caught up to her. He looked fresher, more intent than the night before. The wrapping on his forearm had been replaced by a new cloth.

"Where are you going?" he said.

In a heightened, nearly animal state of awareness, Eliana's hackles shot up. "Nowhere."

"Don't go," he said. "The jungle is a dangerous place."

"I can protect myself from a few birds," she said and felt foolish saying it. She had no survival training. She didn't even know how to fish. She chided herself for not learning more basic skills while she was here, but kept walking.

"It's not the wild animals you have to worry about," Rakulo said. His voice dropped to a whisper. "You'll never make it through the Wall alone."

She froze. "What wall?"

He put his fingers to his lips, glanced around. "Let me guide you. Please."

Eliana hesitated. "How did you know I was leaving?" she asked.

"I heard you gathering food."

She felt her face flush. "You heard me?"

"You make a lot of noise."

She sighed. It didn't take a big leap of imagination to see why she might need a guide. "Okay," she said. "You can come. But I'm leaving now."

"No," he said. "It's not safe. We'll leave at night so they can't track us."

"What do I do until then?"

"Act normal. I'll come find you after dark."

Rakulo walked away, peering carefully around corners and into shadowed alcoves, on the lookout like a man under watch.

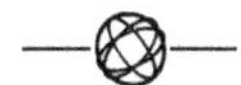

Eliana thought, *Normal... Right. What now?*

She returned to her hut and settled in to wait. The lack of sleep was catching up to her. Without meaning to, she dozed off for a while.

As evening approached, she woke thirsty and drained the remainder of one of the water skins she had prepared for her journey. She got up with the intention of heading to the stream nearby to refill it. But before she made it out the door, she realized that filling the water skin would look suspicious. The skins were meant for outings, and she was supposed to be acting like she wasn't going anywhere.

It would be more natural to fill one of the water jugs Ixchel had given her for use in her hut. She picked up the smallest narrow-necked vessel.

The trip down the quiet, shaded path to the cool stream soothed Eliana. She passed a few women carrying wet laundry back to the village. They were laughing. She smiled at them, and they smiled back. She encountered no one else on the way, and at the stream she found herself alone.

Eliana set the pot down and splashed water on her face from a clear, calm eddy. She raised her face and closed her eyes. She breathed in the earthen smells of moss and mud and let the water drip down her warm skin. She heard no warning sounds until he was upon her.

Hands gripped her hair and shoved her face into the shallow stream. Her front teeth banged into rocks in the stream bed. She inhaled to scream, but water and mud washed into her mouth. She choked. River muck coated her tongue and palate as she struggled for air.

She swung her hands behind her, trying vainly to reach her attacker. One hand found a thick, hairy ankle near her head. She dug her nails in, but that had no effect. She turned her head. Sharp pain lanced into her scalp as hair was torn from its roots. Her lips found ankle bone—or maybe an Achilles tendon. She bit down with all her might.

Her attacker let go as Eliana's teeth drew blood. She scrambled back onto dry land, coughing and gasping for air.

Her attacker snarled and came at her again. She caught her first full glimpse of the man. He wore a mask depicting the gaping maw of a serpent, the mask of Snake from the storytelling. His massive frame and heavily tattooed upper torso gave him away.

Chief Dambu advanced on her with startling speed, drawing an obsidian knife from his belt. Eliana kicked out as the knife came down. A stroke of luck connected her foot squarely with his wrist and sent the knife spinning into the bushes. He fell on her again, pummeling her with his fists and overpowering her with his greater size and strength. She raised her arms to protect herself, but they were battered down relentlessly. She curled up into the fetal position to protect her head and body from the rain of fists.

When Eliana had stopped fighting back, Dambu reached down, seized her ankles with both hands, and dragged her toward the water again. She loosed a full-throated scream and kicked her legs. His fingers slipped on her wet skin, and he lost hold of one ankle. Eliana bucked and rolled over. He snatched for her legs and yanked on her, but in that moment of freedom she managed to reach out and grasp hold of the clay jug. Dambu dragged her through the sand back to the water. Eliana had learned in a self-defense class once that a woman's thighs are her strongest muscle group. As Dambu repositioned himself over her so that he might resume her drowning, she pulled her knees in and thrust outward, landing a solid kick with both feet to the broad target of his chest. Thrown off balance, he staggered backward. Eliana jumped to her feet and swung the jug in both hands, using the fullest arc possible, to strike his head with the vessel.

The clay pot crashed into Dambu's head and shattered. He fell back into the stream.

Shards of pottery floated in the water beside his head, but he remained still.

16
LEAP OF FAITH

"THAT'S AS CLOSE as we're going to get," Reuben said as he flicked the energy output graph onto a wall with a gesture. He expanded its edges until the jagged line, like a heart-rate monitor, was superimposed atop the cumulative output of Eliana's translocation.

Amon compared the two.

"You can't shave off that energy spike in the warm-up phase?" he asked, stepping into the leg of a spacesuit.

"Now that we're filtering the power through the carbonado solution, the bootup procedure is erratic. This is as close as we're going to get right now. If we had a chance to run more simulations, or extra time to tinker with the software..."

"All right," Amon said. "What's the estimated margin of error for the translocation?"

"Give or take a couple miles."

Amon pursed his lips. They had a version of this conversation several times in the harried hours since they'd started playing guess and check to duplicate Eliana's translocation.

"Dangerous proposition," Amon said.

"I'm worried about far more than accuracy. We've never done this before."

The meteorite sample warped and amplified the energy output of the machine in ways Amon would not have believed were possible if he hadn't run the tests himself. The meteorite sample might look and act like a carbonado under Audrey's microscope, but properly interfaced with the Hopper's power source, it served as a superconductor.

As if to remind him precisely how much was on the line for this endeavor to succeed, the grinding sound of the drill steadily chewing through the blast door paused for a moment.

And started back up.

An incoming call dialogue blinked on the computer screen. Amon had muted the ringtone hours ago.

"That's got to be the fiftieth time they've tried to call," Amon said.

"They really want to talk to you," Reuben said. "Maybe they're having trouble with the drill."

"They should have breached the blast door hours ago. It's steel, but it's not impenetrable. They're planning something."

Reuben grunted and turned back to the control unit.

Amon zipped up the spacesuit and ran diagnostics on the oxygen and pressurization systems.

His gaze rose to the graphs on the wall, and his mind spun through the calculations they'd triple and quadruple checked, scouring their formulas for errors and omissions. He found none, but that didn't mean they weren't there.

The drill on the outside of the blast door had been grinding relentlessly for the last day while he and Reuben worked on the machine. They wrestled the laws of physics and the Hopper's software with the kind of relentless determination mustered only by the mad and the desperate.

The drill stopped. Amon involuntarily tensed his whole body in the silence that followed. The spacesuit weighed heavily on him like a full-body anchor, though it weighed only twenty-five pounds, a tenth of the mass of the A7L spacesuit worn by the astronauts of *Apollo 11* on their first mission to the moon.

Amon lifted his chin. What he was about to undertake was no mundane lunar landing.

He and Reuben could only discern limited details about the final destination of Eliana's translocation with the data they had. If he reassembled on an exoplanet like Mars with little or no atmosphere, the suit's life-support system would protect his delicate human composition. If he came out on a planet that did have atmosphere, the suit would do a chemical analysis of the air and tell him if it was safe to breathe. If, however, he came out too close to a star or a black hole...well, if that happened the suit was worthless and he was fucked regardless.

That was a risk he was willing to take. He'd come too far to be scared off by *what-if* scenarios. He had no *what ifs* left. Only *when*.

Only now.

He fitted the sleek helmet over his head and snapped it into place, sealing it with the suit. He slid the outer visor up then touched the computer screen to answer the call.

"Hello?"

He picked up the transponder, cranked the speaker volume so he could hear it through the helmet, and strode to the translocation platform while Fowler's voice echoed around the lab.

"Last chance, Amon," she said. "If you don't open the door now, we will."

"Try not to blow your fingers off when you do it. Firecrackers are dangerous," he said.

"Do you really think..." she began. Background noise rustled through the speaker as people moved around on the other end. Fowler's voice faded into the background.

"Amon, listen to her," Lucas said. "It's the only sensible option."

A few moments passed before Amon recovered from his surprise at hearing Lucas on the other end of the line. He was trying to remember the last time they'd spoken. It had been at least a couple weeks. As usual, Amon had been so absorbed with his mission that he hardly noticed until now.

"Lucas," he said. "How are you?"

"Listen, Amon, this has gone on way too long."

"I'm only doing what I have to do."

"There are other options," Lucas said.

"I thought you'd be on my side in this."

Only silence at the familiar stonewall of their opposing viewpoints.

"Are you and Wes working well together?" Amon asked. "It's been almost two months now."

Amon heard the smile in Lucas's voice. "Well, you know Wes. He's difficult for the sake of being so, but I think he has the company's best interests at heart."

"And how's the company recovering? I don't find much time to check the stats these days."

"Our core business has stabilized somewhat. Solar panel orders are coming in again, so we have positive cash flow. The investors have calmed down, though I'll tell you they'd be a heck of a lot happier if you'd come back to your senses and give up this whole thing. This mess with the meteorite sample isn't good for business."

Amon exchanged a glance with Reuben. "Say, did you ever hear from Dr. Badeux?" he said.

A pause. "I did," Lucas said. "He told me his hands are tied until you agree to cooperate."

Like a big puzzle, Amon began to see how the pieces scattered across the board might fit together.

"How did you know about the meteorite sample, Lucas?" Amon asked.

"Libby told me." He stumbled over the words as they spilled out.

"Libby?"

"I mean, Agent Fowler."

"On a first-name basis now, are we?

No answer.

"They don't work for the FBI, do they, Lucas?"

For the longest time, he hadn't been able to see how the pieces fit, but as with any problem he attacked for long enough, the lines and dots began to connect, the edges started to match up: not being able to get ahold of the Dr. Badeux or anyone in charge at the LTA, the threats against Reuben and Charlie, being tracked to the NASA facility in a record-breaking amount of time.

"You've been working with Fowler this whole time," Amon said.

Lucas responded in a deadpan tone. "Of course, we've been cooperating with the FBI in whatever way they need us to."

"Bullshit. That's not what I mean, and you know it."

Someone covered the microphone on the other end. Amon heard muffled, argumentative voices through the speakers. The call disconnected.

"Fuckin' *gonif* rat!" Reuben said.

They heard a slow hissing, then a burst of bright orange sparks that burned continuously and filled the room with thick plumes of greasy smoke.

"Dammit," Amon said. "Thermite charges." He raised his hand and rolled his pointer finger, the cue for Reuben to boot up the Translocator. Reuben raised his arms in a sharp motion, using the gesture controls to activate the machine.

The steel blast door spat sparks from its center. Through the haze of smoke, Amon could see small blazing cracks extending toward each other until they met in a rough circle. Safer and more clever than trying to use a brute-force blast to remove a door built to withstand it, thermite would chew through a block of solid steel in seconds if properly directed. The drill must have been used to establish optimum positioning for the thermite charges.

Of course, thermite was also a military-grade weapon. Nearly impossible to get ahold of without the right connections. Another piece of the puzzle snapped into place.

The fountains of sparks ceased. A cloud of smoke obscured the door.

"Reuben, open up the relay script," Amon said. He rattled off a series of instructions. Reuben switched over to the keyboard and typed rapidly as he spoke.

Reuben's fingers ceased typing for a moment. "You'll give him a what?" he asked.

"You heard me."

"You hate cameras."

"I know."

A slow, steady banging drummed into the room from the other side of the blast door. Reuben's fingers flew over the keys again as he finished Amon's message. He hit *Enter* to send it.

"Also, get in touch with Mather & Mayberry if something happens. They have my will."

"You're coming back," Reuben grumbled. "With Eliana."

"Thanks, old friend. I hope so."

Reuben nodded. Worry lines creased his brow. His wispy gray hair clung to his sweaty forehead. They looked at each other across the room.

As the Hopper warmed up, another gigantic thud crashed into the blast door. The massive, rough-edged disc of steel that had been cut by the thermite charges tilted out and slammed to the floor.

Reuben waved his arms wildly, working the control unit as fast as he could. Amon held his ground before the sphere of alloy rings on the transfer platform, halfway up the ramp.

Two dozen mercenaries armed to the teeth and dressed in black body armor swarmed through the opening of the blast door and the dissipating cloud of smoke. They fanned out with semiautomatic rifles drawn. The word *HAWKWOOD* was printed across their chests in white letters. In place of the K was a silhouette of a knight chess piece, the outline of a horse's head.

Amon gazed down the row of rifle muzzles. The tactical team stopped below the ramp, far enough away not to be accidentally pulled through during the jump—he hoped. With his free hand, Amon tapped a button on the computer set into the wrist of his spacesuit, ordering it to transmit his voice through the lab's surround-sound speakers so he could be heard. He raised his hands in the universal sign of surrender.

"Move away from the machine!" Fowler cried as she stepped into the lab.

Montoya slinked in behind her. He couldn't keep a smirk off his face, like he'd been dreaming of this day for weeks. He raised his pistol and put Amon in his sights.

"Have I given you reason to fear me, Ms. Fowler?" Amon asked.

"Never hurts to be careful."

Amon held the transponder in one hand. The whole lab shook with a great tremor as the carbonado solution ratcheted the energy that thrummed through the machine's great arch up a notch. The high-pitched keening of the Hopper rose into the air, and transformed into a banshee's screech.

Almost there, he thought.

"Down on your knees, Amon," Fowler said, though her words were inaudible.

"Or what?" he shouted back.

At a glance from Fowler, Montoya shifted the aim of his handgun from Amon to Reuben. Reuben raised his hands and stepped back from the control unit, casting a glance at Amon. The look on Reuben's face told Amon that the translocation had been initiated. No one in the room who could stop it had any intention of doing so now.

Finally, Lucas stepped through the opening in the blast door. He wore a trim blue suit. His once dark-and-curly beard was almost entirely shot through with gray.

"Ah, hello, Reuben," Lucas shouted over the noise. "It took courage coming here after you were warned of the consequences for helping Amon. It's too bad what that means for Charlie."

"If you hurt him, I'll kill you," Reuben said, taking three quick steps toward him.

"Ah-ah-ah," Montoya said. "Wouldn't do that if I were you, pal."

"Amon," Lucas said. "The game is over. You've lost."

"This isn't a game."

"You and I both know you're chasing shadows. Let me help you accept the inevitable. She's dead, Amon. Eliana died on the night of the demonstration, and you killed her."

"Go to hell," Amon said. He glanced back. The alloy rings had been engulfed by a sphere of light. He felt its force like a tangible thing, tugging gently at his body as it pulsed and swirled. His fingers began to tingle, though he was still several feet away.

"Go," Reuben said. "Go now!"

Montoya turned his head to look at the platform. In the instant he glanced away, Reuben closed the distance between them and roared. He grabbed Montoya's pistol with both hands. One shot discharged. Reuben's momentum took them both to the ground.

Amon stepped back.

"Take him down!" Fowler yelled at the team of mercenaries who surrounded Amon. Their fear of the Translocator was evident in their stony faces. They stepped closer, but none set foot on the ramp leading up to the platform.

With a curse, Fowler drew her own handgun from a shoulder holster and pointed it at Amon. His heart skipped a beat as Montoya's gun went off again, locked somewhere between them in the struggle, and Reuben cried out in pain.

Amon turned and sprinted up the ramp as fast as the spacesuit would allow. Another shot fired, and Amon heard a hiss of air as Fowler's bullet opened a hole in his oxygen tank.

The radiant sphere gripped him when it felt his body at the edge of its reach. It pulled. Amon barely remembered to reach up and slam down the radiation visor of his helmet as he was yanked into the light.

17
SECOND SACRIFICE

WHILE DAMBU LAY unconscious, Eliana rummaged for his knife in the bushes. When she found it, her hands steadied as they gripped the obsidian handle.

When she turned back around, Dambu's prone form lay still on the riverbank. Eliana held the knife before her and advanced with murderous intent.

Dambu's deep chest rose ever so slightly. The water was shallow enough where he had fallen that it covered his ears but still allowed him to breathe through his nose and mouth. She nudged him with her toe to make sure he was still out. He didn't move.

She kneeled down in the eddy. A gash in his forehead seeped into the muddied water. She could smell his rancid breath, feel its heat against her forearm as she rested the edge of the obsidian blade on his exposed neck.

I could end it right here, she thought. *Right now. How easy it would be to cut his throat in the water, to end the life of the man who has caused me so much pain and suffering.*

She hesitated. Eliana had never before had such thoughts, and they scared her.

She heard a sudden pattering of feet followed by shouts of approaching people. She took the knife away without drawing blood. Had they heard sounds of the struggle? Had they heard Eliana's desperate shrieks? They were coming down the trail leading from the village, and their footsteps grew louder by the moment.

Eliana had no desire to face them, whoever they were. None would take kindly to an assault on their chief, no matter who attacked whom first. If the wrong person arrived, like one of the young men who was loyal to Dambu, the ones who wanted to be warriors like him, then the scene arrayed before them would not work in her favor. When he returned to consciousness, it would his word against hers. Would they believe Eliana had bested this brute of a man without using the element of surprise to her advantage?

Dambu groaned and began to stir. Eliana turned the knife and smashed the butt of the handle into his forehead. He returned to stillness.

She spearheaded into the jungle perpendicular to the river and away from the main trail so as not to be seen by whoever was coming toward her. If she didn't get lost again, she could walk half a mile out and swing back toward the village, grab her rucksack, and get as far away from here as possible.

If she wandered off track, like she had before, she would come across the stone city of *Uchben Na*. Sunlight faded quickly in the jungle and it would be full dark in a matter of minutes. *I have enough memories of* Uchben Na *in the night to last me a lifetime,* she thought, *so I better be careful.*

Fifty yards into the woods, Eliana ducked behind a thick tree and peered back. Pattering feet slapped against the packed dirt of the trail, and then two men burst into view. The men cried out and ran to Dambu's side.

Ixchel came into view next. When she saw her husband, she did not cry out. Eliana saw her jaw muscles clench in anger, and then she, too, kneeled by his side.

At that moment, a flash of lightning and an enormous crack of thunder lit the dim sky. Eliana jumped up, turning in the direction of *Uchben Na,* where the flash seemed to have originated.

Could it be?

She hurled herself toward the jungle and ran for *Uchben Na* and the source of that light. The hope that she had lost once again swelled in her heart as she dodged through the brush while Ixchel found her husband and chief lying in the water, bleeding from his head. From the broken pottery, she was certain to know who had felled her husband.

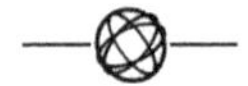

At first, Amon operated under the belief that he had materialized in the cold emptiness of dead space, his worst nightmare come to pass. A sense of weightlessness permeated his body from the disorientation of the jump, and no noise reached his ears within the spacesuit, save for the sound of his own breathing.

While his eyes adjusted, the nausea hit him like a gut shot. He recognized the sick feeling as the effect of the molecular reassembly process, or what he and Reuben called the space bends. It was worse than usual—much worse.

As he focused on his breathing, he looked up. The stars above him twinkled in a deep-purple blanket of sky.

Which meant atmosphere. Which meant he was on a planet after all. The light was sparse enough to be the forerunner to dawn or the afterglow of dusk. He couldn't tell which.

He picked a boot up and set it back down. Gravity seemed to be about the same as Earth gravity. That was a positive sign as well.

Reuben would be immensely pleased with himself if he knew Amon had arrived safely. But Amon couldn't activate the transponder to relay the message until he found Eliana.

Amon looked around. He seemed to be standing on the set of an Indiana Jones movie. Vast structures of stone lined the edges of an open courtyard, and a stepped pyramid jutted into the fading light of the violet sky.

It was only as he gazed around, trying to orient himself in the surreal environment, that he felt a tightness in his chest and remembered the air hissing out of his oxygen tank before he'd been pulled into the translocation platform.

He tapped the computer on his forearm with a gloved finger so he could switch over to the reserve oxygen tank, but the electronics were dead. Either the bullet that had breached his oxygen tank somehow short-circuited the electronics in the suit as well, or the superconducting translocation yanked the juice out of the battery that powered the life-support system within the sealed spacesuit.

Either way, he was almost out of air.

The second wave of nausea slammed into him. His knees buckled, the sky and the ground switched places, and the world jolted as his helmet bounced off the floor.

The plastic visor did its job, not so much as denting from the impact.

Amon lay on his side while red splotches decorated his vision. He rolled back, but the bulky life-support systems prevented any comfort he might have gained from that position. Panting heavily now, he struggled to his knees and gripped the helmet in his gloved hands. He tried to release the locking mechanism and turn the helmet, but it was stuck.

Noticing a tight-knit group of people creeping across the courtyard, Amon waved for help. They huddled together as if he were a predator to be approached with caution and extreme trepidation.

He staggered toward them. They retreated back. More people arrived at a run. They formed a loose ring around him. He realized that the layer of gold coating his helmet, which was designed to protect him from the sun's radiation in space, also prevented them from seeing his face.

So they couldn't know when he started gasping for air, unable to communicate, that inside the spacesuit he was suffocating.

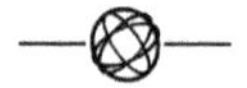

By the time Eliana reached the courtyard of *Uchben Na*, a small group of people had already gathered. They had their backs to her. She slowed her steps as she approached them. Her chest heaved. She tucked the obsidian knife into the waist of her tunic so that it was out of sight but within easy reach.

The sun hid completely behind the great pyramid now, and stars had begun to speckle the deepening violet firmament. The two moons were nearly kissing again, looming large over the city and casting their silver and pale-scarlet light upon it.

She pushed her way into the crowd. Citlali was there, and Eliana saw the fear that hollowed her eyes.

"Are you okay?" Citlali asked when she saw Eliana. "What happened to your face?"

Eliana shook her head and squeezed past Citlali into the circle. In the middle she saw a figure lying on its side on the stone and grass floor. It was clothed from head to foot in synthetic cloth, with a helmet covering its head. Like Xucha. Except this one's garments were bulkier, and white—the white of a spacesuit.

Eliana fell to her knees and lifted the helmet in her hands. Putting her face close to the gold-coated visor, she was able to see through it.

She saw Amon. His face was peaceful, as if he was sleeping. His eyelids fluttered. He smiled when he saw her then opened his mouth to speak. No words came out. Instead, his eyes bulged, and he choked.

"Amon!" she cried. Eliana gripped the helmet with both hands and twisted. It didn't budge. She tried turning in the other direction. It didn't give.

"Help," she said, beckoning to Citlali. "Please help me."

Citlali shook her head and took a step back, afraid of what she thought she knew. Eliana cried out in anger, "He can't breathe! Help me!" No one moved. They just stared at her.

Eliana looked around the gathering of scared faces. Too much tragedy had befallen them. They were all afraid to be the one who caused the wrath of the gods to bear down upon their people again. They had been conditioned to inaction.

Giving up on any chance of aid, she searched frantically for a latch on the helmet, some kind of release mechanism. She found one, but even with the lock depressed, the helmet was sealed tightly. She pulled hard counter-clockwise, and her sweaty palms slipped against the plastic bubble.

"Come on!" she screamed. She slammed the palm of her hand on the ground in frustration.

That's when she saw the reflection in the visor.

She looked up. The crowd had parted. Dambu shambled forward. Blood dripped down his neck and shoulders. He carried a melon-sized rock in one hand. Eliana struggled harder with the helmet. The muscles in her hands spasmed and seized. Her fingernail broke when it caught a crack in helmet, and a sharp pain shot into her finger.

Dambu raised the rock in his hand. When his arm reached its apex, a soft vibrating noise caused him to pause. From out of the jungle, a metallic orb floated. The crowd parted on the other side and stepped back even farther. The orb halted between Dambu and Eliana, and Xucha appeared.

"I knew you would come," Dambu said. "You're so predictable."

"You disobeyed me," Xucha said. "I told you this woman must not be harmed."

Citlali and the group of gathered natives scattered back, giving Xucha and his orb a wider berth. Some fell to their knees and mumbled prayers under their breath. Others wrung their hands and hastily retreated toward the village, glancing over their shoulders as they ran.

Eliana finally managed to rotate Amon's helmet a few degrees. A sucking noise released the seal, and fresh air rushed into his suit. He gasped as oxygen flowed into his lungs, his chest heaving under Eliana's hand.

Dambu feinted toward her.

As she instinctively reached up and felt for the ring around her neck, Eliana realized that it was missing. The twine necklace must have come loose in the struggle with Dambu.

When she looked back up, a glow pulsed from Dambu's empty hand.

"Looking for this?" he said. Without hesitation, he lifted his arm and tossed Eliana's ring across the courtyard. It soared through the air and landed among the cracked paving stones behind the gathered villagers with a soft jingle, and harmlessly discharged a bolt of violent energy with a flash.

The snake projection on the face of Xucha's helmet hissed, its tongue lashing out. Xucha raised his fist and clenched it.

Dambu reacted faster. Instead of attacking Xucha, he cocked his arm and launched the melon-sized rock at the orb behind him. His aim was true. The rock clanged off metal, denting it, and the orb wobbled as it careened through the air in a downward spiral.

Dambu leaped out and seized the metal sphere, then lifted both hands over his head and hurled it to the ground. It ricocheted with a hollow metallic echo, bounced, and clattered across the paving stones. The image of Xucha flickered then vanished.

"A hologram," she heard Amon whisper.

Dambu turned to Eliana. "Your stone is gone. Xucha's demon is dead. No one will protect you now."

Eliana gripped Amon under his arms and tried to drag him back with her. But he was too heavy. Amon reached a gloved hand out and gripped her leg weakly. She dared not leave his side. Even facing death, she dared not leave him ever again.

"No," said Rakulo, stepping from the crowd to block his father's way. "It's not her fault."

Dambu stared at his son. "Do you think that matters? Xucha is not dead. He will return for his demon *and* for retribution. Eliana's death is the only way to fight back."

"It's not the only way."

"Please, Dambu," Ixchel said, stepping up next to her son. "We have already lost too many. If you do this, Xucha will bring a new plague down upon us. What hope will there be then?"

"What hope is there now? Step aside," he growled.

Rakulo shoved his father back. Dambu drove his elbow into his son's face then threw him to the ground. Ixchel bowed her head and stepped aside.

Before Rakulo could rise, Dambu rushed Eliana, a predatory snarl of rage twisting his face. Amon, who had thus far remained prone on his back at Eliana's side, kicked out his booted feet and tangled them with Dambu's legs. The chief toppled and fell onto Eliana, his hands extending and reaching as if to tear out her throat. His meaty fingers surrounded her neck at the same time as she withdrew her hands from her tunic and raised the obsidian knife into Dambu's exposed ribs. His eyes widened as he fell onto his own blade.

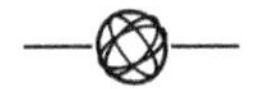

"Eliana," Amon said weakly. His ankle throbbed where it had been twisted. The big man's body pinned his wife to the ground a few yards away.

Amon tried to rise on unsteady feet, but dozens of people fell on the three tangled bodies and knocked him back down. The press of flesh reverberated with angry shouts. Amon roared and forced himself to his knees, then his feet, clawing and digging his way deeper into the pile where Eliana was still trapped.

More people piled on, blocking out the moonlight. Though the hard upper torso of the spacesuit prevented him from being crushed, it became difficult to breathe. His vision swam.

A commanding voice rang out. As quickly as the dozens had swarmed in, the pressure began to recede. Amon was eventually extricated from the pile and righted by a teenage boy.

The commanding voice belonged to him, the same youth who had tried to resist the big man before he attacked Eliana. The youth's square jaw jutted forward in a hard line as he continued to pull people off of the pile. His nose was a bloody mess, but he seemed not to notice, and not noticing gave him an even fiercer aspect. The youth stared down any who questioned his commands without flinching. Those who might have disagreed with him first glanced to the middle-aged woman standing at the youth's shoulder then seemed to change their minds. For some reason, the presence of the two together carried authority.

Calm and order returned to the gathering as Eliana and the big man were revealed on the ground. With the help of the teenage boy, Amon lifted the big man off his wife.

Kneeling by Eliana's side, Amon pressed his hands against her blood-spattered torso, frantically searching for the source of the blood. A young woman tried to approach them but Amon glared at her. He might even have growled.

Despite the blood, Amon found no major wounds. Her face was beginning to swell, and she had many minor scrapes and bruises, but nothing life-threatening that he could find. A wave of relief washed over him, followed by a lance of guilt. He cupped her slack face in his gloved hands. She was staring at him but saying nothing.

"Eliana," he said. "Eliana, it's me."

"Amon," she said. "Am I dead?"

"Not a chance."

"I thought I was dead for a minute."

"You're very much alive."

"You came."

"Of course I did," Amon said. "I never stopped looking for you."

"How long has it been? What month is it? What day is it today?"

"I think it's a Thursday? Middle of September. Or maybe October. I don't know. I haven't really been keeping track."

She laughed, a glorious musical sound, and marveled at the mundaneness of the date.

"A Thursday in September," she said. Then, "You saved me."

"Looks like you saved yourself," Amon replied, looking to the side.

She glanced over at the big man. Her face went pale. Gripping Eliana's hands, Amon could feel her begin to shake.

The teenage boy and the middle-aged woman now kneeled at the big man's side. Moonlight glinted off an obsidian blade protruding from his chest.

18
THE WELL OF SACRIFICES

ELIANA REGAINED HER feet with a grunt of effort and held a hand to her side where the handle of the knife had left a deep bruise.

She took a few uncertain steps toward the chief where he lay dying. Amon stopped her with a hand on her arm.

"What are you doing?"

"It's okay," she said. "You'll see."

Amon looked around uncertainly. "At least help me get out of this damned spacesuit first."

Eliana unzipped the spacesuit, dropped the pieces on the ground, and helped him climb out of it. Urging her to wait another moment, Amon left her side long enough to hunt for something amid the grass beyond where the several hundred villagers now gathered in the courtyard.

He returned with an oblong metal object in his hand and held a button at the top of it until an indicator light turned a steady orange. "It's a transponder," he explained. "It will take a little while for Reuben to activate the Hopper from his side, but when he does this light will turn green."

"How long?" she asked.

"Hopefully, not long. He's supposed to power up the Hopper once an hour to check for incoming signals."

Eliana heard a hint of doubt in his voice, but she had other concerns at the moment so she just nodded. Amon hovered protectively behind her as she approached Dambu. Rakulo and Ixchel kneeled at the chief's side.

"Don't waste this opportunity," Dambu said, looking into his son's face. "Trade my life for another lunar cycle."

"I don't want to be chief," Rakulo said.

"We are not always given a choice, my son."

"We should be."

Dambu laid his head back against the ground and closed his eyes. Rakulo stifled a sob, covering his mouth with a hand. He made a gesture, and immediately a half dozen of Dambu's warriors bent down and lifted the dying chief on their shoulders. They carried him out of the city, and the crowd of villagers trickled from the courtyard of *Uchben Na* after them.

Before following, Rakulo turned to Citlali. "My father's sacrifice has given us more than another cycle of the moons," he said, his voice regaining its tone of command as he spoke. "But he was right. Xucha lives, and he will return for his demon. Hide it deep among the ruins."

Citlali acquiesced with a nod in her usual laconic manner, lifted the dented metal orb from where it rested among the weeds, and disappeared into the dark city of crumbling stones.

The first time Eliana saw them carry a body out of *Uchben Na,* she had stayed behind. This time, she went with them. Rakulo, Ixchel, Eliana, and Amon trailed the procession down a paved white path into the jungle. Amon walked beside her. He intertwined his fingers with hers, and she held on tight.

"What's happening?" Amon asked. "What did they say to each other?"

"I don't know if I fully understand it myself," Eliana said. "I need to see this first."

The flat, paved road of white stones led to a deep well. The water it contained glowed a sickly green in the night. Eliana stared, transfixed by the strangeness of it. The open hole in the earth was a hundred feet across with the surface of the water thirty feet below ground level.

The *cenote* steamed slightly and gave off a pungent sulfur stench. Some bodies of water on Earth contained luminescent bacteria, but for some reason Eliana didn't get the feeling that the glow in this one was entirely natural.

Rakulo kneeled at his father's side again where the villagers had set him down on an outcropping of stone. He wrapped his fingers around the hilt of the obsidian knife in Dambu's chest. Ixchel put her hands on Rakulo's shoulders and turned her face to the night sky. Tears streamed down her cheeks.

Ixchel and Rakulo said a prayer over Chief Dambu's body. The assembled villagers raised their hands in the A-okay sign.

Rakulo yanked the knife from his father's ribcage with a squelching sound. Dambu gurgled, and the life faded from his eyes. Rakulo looked back at his mother. Ixchel gestured for him to proceed.

"I will sacrifice him," Rakulo said, "but not the old way."

Instead of plunging the obsidian knife back into his father's chest and removing his heart, Rakulo wiped the blade on the grass and held it up in the moonlight for all to see.

"Xucha's demon controls those who displease him—with this," he said, "with human sacrifice. My father was fighting for our freedom." He met Eliana's gaze. "I saw father speaking to Xucha in the jungle last night. With a single gesture, Xucha caused the greatest warrior among us to fall to his knees, writhing in agony. But tonight, our chief proved that with cunning and intelligence, even Xucha can be defeated. This knife no longer belongs to Xucha. It belongs to us. *We* choose what to do with it now."

So Rakulo had seen it, too, Eliana thought.

"What is he saying?" Amon asked. "They look so angry."

"Rakulo is saying they're going to fight back. The religion is a mechanism for the gods to enforce control over these people. When it failed, that mechanical orb thing and hologram you saw was sent in to hurt them. It has some kind of powers that I don't understand."

"You mean the gods are real?" Amon said. He looked worried.

Eliana just pursed her lips and nodded. "You saw it, same as I did."

Rakulo approached Eliana. Lowering his voice, he said to her, "I never thought my father would hurt you. I am truly sorry. But, you see, it was not you he was fighting against."

Eliana nodded. "I think I understand. I forgive him."

"Thank you," Rakulo said.

"You're right, though," Eliana said. "It's your choice to make."

Rakulo nodded and tucked the obsidian blade into his tunic at the waist. "But at what cost?"

He turned away when a low humming sound drifted from the edge of the trees surrounding the *cenote*. He stared into the forest for a long moment, then slowly walked back to his father's body. With the help of three others, Rakulo cast Dambu's body into the phosphorescent depths. It made a splash as it entered the water, floated for a moment, and then the water pulsed and swarmed with particles that dissolved the flesh in a matter of moments.

"Were those piranha?" Amon asked.

Eliana didn't think so. She shook her head. "The offering was accepted," she whispered.

The low humming sound faded into the distance, and Eliana saw Rakulo relax his shoulders slightly.

The *Kakuli* people meandered back into their village, saddened by the night's loss, confused by what they had learned, and unconcerned by what would happen to Eliana next.

She couldn't blame them.

In the courtyard of *Uchben Na*, on their way back to the village, the transponder signal light turned green. Amon exhaled heavily, an obvious sigh of relief.

"We're going home," he said.

Eliana nodded and turned to Rakulo and Ixchel, who had remained behind. A moment later, Citlali crossed the courtyard and approached them.

"It's hidden," she told Rakulo, who nodded.

"So what happens next?" Eliana asked.

Rakulo frowned. "I don't know. Xucha may still punish us for my father's actions."

"Why? He got a sacrifice like he wanted."

"Who can understand the whims of the gods?"

"Maybe he will allow your people to live in peace. Maybe the sacrifices can end now," Eliana said, though even as the words came out she didn't believe that it would be that easy.

Rakulo shook his head. "What if we don't feed the gods before the next full moons, and my people fall sick again?"

"Spoken like a true chief. Your people would do well to have such a caring leader."

"I know what happens to chiefs."

"So what will you do?"

"I'll go to him. Xucha will come looking for his demon, and show me a way through the Wall."

Eliana frowned. He had mentioned a wall before, but she didn't fully understand the reference.

"Eliana," Amon said, pointing at a bright pinprick of light that had appeared in the air. It slowly grew more vibrant. Light beams poked out in several directions at variegated levels of brightness and reach until a rough sphere about six feet in diameter illuminated *Uchben Na*.

Rakulo, Ixchel, and Citlali stared, transfixed. This must have seemed like magic to them, too.

Eliana hugged Rakulo. "You would have been a good guide," she said. "I'm sorry we never got to take that journey together."

Rakulo nodded, pursing his lips. "Be safe."

She hugged Citlali next. "Thank you for teaching me and letting me into your home."

With a shy smile, she responded simply, "You're welcome. Goodbye."

Finally, Eliana turned to Ixchel. "I'm so sorry for your loss. I wish we had met under different circumstances."

"Me, too," Ixchel said.

"What will you do next?"

"I will mourn my husband, and teach my son to be a good chief."

"Thank you for being kind to me when I needed it."

"You're most welcome."

Eliana turned away from the three of them and took Amon's hand. As they approached the sphere of light, something glinted on the ground and caught Eliana's attention. It was her ring, lying forgotten among the paving stones where Dambu had tossed it.

Amon realized what it was as well. "You can't take that with you," he said. "We have no way to isolate the carbonado. It will interfere with the translocation."

Leaving Amon's side, she picked it up and walked over to Rakulo.

"This helped me. Perhaps it will be of some use to you."

Rakulo took hold of the ring carefully.

"Here," Ixchel said. "A gift for you in return." She removed her beautiful necklace of turquoise stones and seashells and draped it around Eliana's neck.

"Thank you," Eliana said.

With one last glance at the faces of her friends, Eliana took Amon's hand, and together they stepped into the light.

19
BREAKING NEWS

AMON FELT LIKE a rookie pilot stumbling out of his first high-G training session in the centrifuge: legs of rubber, stomach in knots. He and Eliana sank to the floor, leaning against each other.

They were inside of the shell of alloy rings surrounding the translocation platform. He peered into the lab, looking for Lucas, Fowler, Montoya, and the rifle-wielding tactical team of mercenaries who had attended his departure. He saw none of them, though a furor of voices resounded through the rough circular hole in the blast door.

Eliana massaged her temples and let her head loll back. She groaned with pleasure. "Air conditioning," she said. "Holy crap that feels good."

"Aren't you nauseated?"

"Yeah. But the air conditioning!"

As Amon was thinking about how he would have to talk to Reuben about finding a way to temper the physical side-effects of the translocation, the man himself shuffled up the ramp into view. A sling held his left arm close to his side.

"Is that your lovely wife?" Reuben said.

"Reuben," Eliana said, sitting up. "What happened to your arm?"

"Got shot."

"He took a bullet for me," Amon said, standing. Reuben drew air through his teeth when Amon embraced him. "You old *putz*."

"Fah!" Reuben said. "You should talk. You don't look so good, yourself actually. But I'm not sure how much longer you-know-who will stay back now that you're here."

"Where's Lucas? What happened?"

"Plenty of time to talk about that later. I'm sorry, I know you hate the cameras. But here comes Carter now."

"Mr. Fisk!" Carter shouted, pushing through the aperture in the blast door and stomping across the room. Laden with crisscrossing camera straps, cradling a digital recorder, a notebook and several other knickknacks in one hand, he snapped photos with a camera.

Ch-chic, ch-chic.

Amon smiled shyly. For once, he was only mildly uncomfortable in front of the lenses. After all, he had brought this on himself.

A cameraman filming video hurried after Carter, followed by dozens of other reporters and photographers. A new media liaison Amon had never seen before wrangled them together and gained control over the initial clamor.

Amon stepped up to answer questions, but most of the questions were directed at his wife.

Eliana smiled gracefully and answered the questions. No, she was unharmed. Yes, the Translocator is perfectly safe—wouldn't she know?

Amon stepped back and let her take the spotlight. She was as elegant and stunning as ever, wearing a coarsely woven cloth, hemp sandals, and a turquoise-and-shell necklace.

"I still can't believe you got shot," said Eliana.

Reuben laughed. "I got lucky. The bullet went straight through. It'll make a good conversation starter though."

"Okay," Amon said. "Tell us from the beginning so Dr. Badeux can hear the story, starting with what happened after I translocated out of the lab."

It had been two days since they returned home. Amon called in a doctor on the first night to care for Eliana's injuries. They had slept fourteen hours straight and spent the following day and night locked in their bedroom together, only cracking the door to order food.

Now, cleaned up and well rested, the group gathered in the living room of Amon's home. He and Eliana sat on the love seat across from Reuben and Audrey on the bigger couch. Dr. Badeux, who had arrived from France an hour ago, sat in the recliner.

"After we sent the message to Carter and Amon went through the Hopper after Eliana," Reuben said, "I dialed Audrey's phone and left the line open. When she heard the gunshots, she called the local cops and the *real* FBI. By the time I had stumbled out of the lab, delirious and bleeding, the authorities had arrived in droves. There was a showdown between the real SWAT team and the private military contractors Lucas hired—Hawkwood, they're called—which Lucas used as a distraction to slip away. But Hawkwood doesn't want to get on the bad side of the authorities or they risk losing their license to operate, so that fizzled out real quick.

"The cops put out an APB for Lucas, but he made it into Mexico through the Laredo border crossing under an assumed identity. The FBI told us yesterday that they have footage of him crossing the border in his car, but that they lost track of him after that. If you ask me, Lucas must have been planning his escape for a while. The whole thing with Hawkwood impersonating FBI agents was just a ruse for him to sidetrack us while he gutted the company's bank accounts."

"Hawkwood lost their security contract with NASA, too," said Audrey. "They're under investigation now."

"Lucas wasn't lying about cash flow problems though," Amon said, pursing his lips. "Fisk Industries was in trouble. But instead of doing something to help, he shut down the Beijing plant, sold off the equipment, and funneled millions of dollars straight into his pocket."

"I never did trust him," Eliana said.

Reuben nodded. "Wes is fervently denying any involvement, of course. He senses which way the wind is blowing, now that Eliana and Amon's faces are all over the news again, and fears about the Translocator's safety have been assuaged."

"Why did Hawkwood agree to go along with Lucas's crazy idea in the first place?" Audrey asked.

"They wanted the Translocator for themselves," Amon said without hesitation. "Can you imagine how dangerous a machine like that would be in the hands of the wrong people?"

"It's our duty to make sure that never happens," Reuben said.

"Money is no object," Dr. Badeux said. "Just tell me what the Auriga Project needs and you'll have it."

"I appreciate that," Amon said. "The engineers and scientists at the lunar colony will, too."

"Your funding will be reinstated immediately, of course. I've already filed the paperwork," Dr. Badeux said, taking off his glasses and rubbing his eyes. "I truly am sorry. Lucas painted a very convincing picture. He said you'd cracked, Amon, after Eliana went missing, and that the best thing for everyone would be to shut the project down. I couldn't argue that logic. With everything else in the media, you can imagine how painful this whole ordeal was for us—not that it holds a candle to what you both went through, of course."

"It's in the past now," Amon said. "I'm just glad we get to pick up where we left off."

"Eliana, what happened to you while you were gone?" Audrey asked. "Reuben tells me that you lived in a primitive village with other people. But how did humans get to another planet in the first place?"

"I don't know how to answer that question, to be perfectly honest. It was like they had been there for several hundred years already, maybe longer. I was so busy trying to survive and learn the language that I didn't really give it much thought."

"So what are you going to do now?"

"Spend some time writing down what happened while it's still fresh in my mind. In a weird way, this might turn out to be the jump-start my archaeology career needed. I've received three job offers since I've been back."

"If you'll excuse me," Amon said, pushing himself up from the couch, "I have to go now, or I'll be late for my 'exclusive interview' with Carter." He used air quotes for the phrase.

Eliana stood and grabbed Amon's hand as he turned to leave. She planted a kiss firmly on his mouth and pulled his hips to hers.

"Wish me luck?" he asked.

"Luck," she said.

"You'll be here when I get back?"

"Are you kidding me? I have a comfortable bed and air conditioning. I'm not leaving this house for a week."

They all laughed.

20
BEYOND THE WALL

ON THE LAST stretch of his three-day hike, Rakulo tightened the straps of his pack, drove his legs into soft earth, and powered up the steep hill to the base of Xucha's Wall.

At the top of the hill, he shook the dirt and leaves out of his sandals and stared up at the vast, seamless slab of Wall. It stretched far above the tallest, most ancient trees, seemingly into the clouds themselves, and as far as his eyes could see to either side. As the Wall extended in both directions from where he stood, it bent back in a concave arc, enfolding the jungle and land it contained.

Rakulo first learned about the existence of Xucha's Wall on a turkey-hunting trip when he was six years old. His father had brought him to where Xucha's Wall met the cliffs in the dead-end canyon at the edge of the southern reach. Dambu explained to his stunned protégé how the Wall encompassed their people's entire area for three days' hike in every direction.

"It surrounds us?"

"Yes."

"How long has it been here?"

"Forever."

"But that's impossible."

"Is it?"

"But why?"

His father stared at him until Rakulo snapped his mouth shut. Instead of chiding him for asking too many questions, Dambu had answered in a whisper, "God knows."

He had meant that literally. As far as Rakulo knew, no man or woman in his village had ever been on the other side of the Wall.

Being an inquisitive child, Rakulo soon came up with a more important question. Since the Wall did not extend into the ocean (that he had seen), why, he wondered, had no one attempted to swim around it?

"I knew a man once who tried that. He never returned. We lost two good men during that cycle."

Rakulo opened his hands and laid them on the Wall, running his fingers along every reachable inch of the smooth slab for several yards in either direction. The stone of the Wall was so different from the great pyramids in *Uchben Na*. It was smooth instead of rough. It seemed to be one continuous piece. There were no bricks, and therefore no gaps between them—nothing for a man to grasp onto. Rain water slid off Xucha's Wall but carved no path through the material. An obsidian knife directed against the Wall would dull before the Wall itself would chip or break. Xucha's Wall seemed to defy the passage of time, to defy nature itself.

Rakulo had long ago given up trying to penetrate the Wall, though he had dreamed of finding a way to the other side of it since he knew it existed.

Before Dambu's death, though he may not have been aware of it at the time, his father had given Rakulo a unique opportunity.

He turned and headed back down the soft dirt hill, leaving a clear trail of heavy footprints to a small grass-filled clearing within sight of the Wall. On the ground in the clearing, he swung his pack down, opened the flap, and withdrew Xucha's demon—a battered sphere made of the same material as his Wall.

It seemed obvious that the two were connected. Today, he was going to find out just how closely related they were.

Rakulo left the demon in the clearing then walked back in the direction of the village. He moved quickly. He did not know how long it would take, but he suspected he did not have much time.

After the demon was out of sight, Rakulo doubled back, walking carefully backward and using a leafy branch as a brush to cover his trail. When he reached a large tree with low branches, he scampered up it, the now-empty pack on his back swinging from side to side as he climbed.

In a bushy intersection of branches, with Xucha's Wall and the demon both in view, he concealed himself and waited.

It didn't take long. What he saw made his skin crawl and his breath quicken. The truth was so much wilder than he had ever dreamed possible.

First, he heard the low humming sound, and then a shiny circular demon came straight *through* the seamless face of Xucha's Wall. It spun around, its dim, red eyes searching for signs of something in the daylight. Finding nothing, it zoomed down the Wall, along the ground, and into the clearing where it circled over its fallen brethren.

Rakulo had to fight to control his breathing and remain still for what he saw next.

At the place where the demon came through the Wall, a hole tall enough to stand in suddenly appeared. One minute it wasn't there, and the next it was. The hole was located above and slightly to the right of where Rakulo's footprints marched up the hill to the base of the Wall, but closer to the ground than where he perched in the tree now.

Beyond the Wall, there were no trees. He saw scorched dirt, reddish brown fading to black, cracked with deep gashes, dry and flaky. Jutting out of the ground in the widest of the cracks, a black needle, mostly obscured from view, stabbed into the purple sky.

Xucha stepped up into the hole and jumped to the ground thirty feet below without breaking his stride. His spherical head reflected the leaves and trees above him as he marched over to the demon.

He stood over it for a moment and cocked his head to the side like a particularly clever turkey staring at a berry used as a lure, as if wondering whether the treat was a trap. Though he had no visible eyes like a man, Rakulo imagined him gazing down at the trail of footprints leading back to *Kakul*.

Please don't follow them, please don't, Rakulo thought.

Xucha bent down, lifted the demon in his arms, and walked back toward the Wall. Rakulo let out a sigh of relief. When Xucha reached the Wall, instead of jumping to the hole he put a foot on the Wall and then walked up it, his body extended horizontally. Rakulo began to quake.

When Xucha and his live demon had moved through the hole, Rakulo's view through the hole faded, and the Wall was once again a seamless, smooth face, slightly curved.

Rakulo waited in his perch until the sun set and darkness descended on the jungle. He didn't count himself fully safe until he had walked for half the night back toward *Kakul*, where he bedded down in a rocky, covered hollow to sleep until the sun rose.

He didn't get much sleep. His fingers caressed the dark stone on the ring around his neck, the one Eliana had given him before she left as mysteriously as she had arrived. While he lay awake, his mind raced with the new knowledge he had gained that day. He wanted desperately to talk to Citlali about it. His entire being cried out that his people had to know the truth.

He was glad for the two days' journey home. It gave him time to quell his excitement and think rationally. Not everyone would believe him. Not yet, anyway. He must talk to those he trusted first, to Citlali and his mother in particular.

When he made it through the Wall and returned to tell the tale, then he could tell everyone. Then they would believe him. Then they would know the truth.

Dear reader,

Thank you for reading *The Auriga Project*!

I hope you enjoyed discovering Kakul as much as I did when I first imagined it.

But this particular story does not end here.

Continue on to *The Alien Element* to find out how Eliana, Amon, and Rakulo fare on their next adventure.

What will Rakulo discover beyond the Wall?

Who will Amon find in his lab?

And what will Eliana do about the ancient mysteries she's uncovered?

The Alien Element picks up where *The Auriga Project* left off. It's full of new twists and surprises, and I know you'll love it.

Get *The Alien Element* today. While you're there, join my SFF book club and score my Starter Library of science fiction stories absolutely free.

www.mgherron.com/tae

Until next time.
Your science fiction adventurer,

MG Herron

ABOUT THE AUTHOR

M.G. Herron is an independent science fiction and fantasy novelist.

Born in Limestone, Maine, USA in 1988 as Matthew Gilbert Herron, he was a reader from a young age, and a world traveler as soon as he could walk. It's been his life's passion to seek new adventures wherever he goes.

After majoring in English Literature at McMaster University, Matt promptly fell off the grid to travel throughout Europe and India. He's also worked as a whitewater rafting guide on the Yellowstone River, swam in a Mayan cenote, and climbed sandstone towers in southern Germany.

When he began writing professionally in 2012, Matt made his way to Austin, TX, where he now lives with his wife, Shelly, and their dog, Elsa.

In addition to publishing books and traveling as much as he can, Matt works with tech startups across the United States as a content strategist, helping them to refine their stories and grow their businesses.

Learn more about Matt and join M.G. Herron's SFF book club at mgherron.com.

ALSO BY M.G. HERRON

TRANSLOCATOR TRILOGY

The Auriga Project (Book 1)
The Alien Element (Book 2)
The Ares Initiative (Book 3)

STANDALONE NOVEL

The Republic

SHORT STORY COLLECTION

Boys & Their Monsters

CPSIA information can be obtained
at www.ICGtesting.com
Printed in the USA
BVHW031826201118
533647BV00001B/85/P